VIDEO GAME ELEMENTARY

TRAPPED IN CLASS

Scott Charles

Yellow Morning Press

First paperback edition January 2022

Paperback ISBN: 978-1-7361521-6-4
Digital ISBN: 978-1-957463-99-5

Illustration copyright © 2022 by Florian Garbay

CONTENTS

1
DOUBLE-UP

"YOU JUST SORT OF TAP IT — *LIKE THIS!*"

Connor's best friend, Glitch, slapped his Vid-Glove against the Potions Machine. There was a loud hiss. A bottle of Double-Up Potion shot into his hand.

"See? Piece of cake," bragged Glitch.

Behind him, the Potions Machine was still hissing. There was a *pop*, and suddenly bottles were launching into the air!

Connor dived across the floor. His arms blurred. He snagged bottle after bottle until he had enough Double-Up Potion to fill one of the high tables next to their lockers.

"Whoops." Glitch smiled sheepishly.

Glitch's real name was Sven Svensen. He was ten years old, same as Connor. He wore a skull cap and swim-goggle glasses.

No one knew why Glitch's Vid-Glove malfunctioned. It just did.

The Vid-Glove was a sort of tube attached to every student's right or left arm. Like cell phones back home, the Vid-Glove had many uses inside the virtual world.

It could send messages. It could display maps and coordinates. It could even store items.

And not just *school* items.

With a tap, Connor summoned his Wolf Buster Sword. He knew he wasn't supposed to, but he couldn't resist. He wanted to grip the sword one more time!

His body thrummed with excitement.

Grinning, he swung the sword in the air.

He really wanted to hunt!

"No swords in the hall, Mr. Lamb," said a teacher in passing.

"Sorry, Mr. G."

Connor banished the sword back to storage. He eyed the Double-Up Potions. He tried to store a few of those, too.

BZZZ!

Connor's Vid-Glove gave a warning shake. Apparently the glitched potions couldn't be stored like regular items.

"Oh man," Connor groaned.

"Now you know how I feel," said Glitch. "My stupid Vid-Glove can't store anything. Speaking of which—" he waved at the potions, "we should probably drink these. Yeah, it's a waste of Hit Points. But I'm not lugging them all the way to Mr. Lively's classroom. There's a *troll* on that route."

Connor laughed.

Together, he and Glitch drained the twelve Double-Up Potions. A warm feeling spread through Connor's avatar, his digitized body, while a message informed him that the potion had no effect on his currently maxed bar of health.

ALERT! Health bar already at maximum.
Your Hit Points did not double.

Oh well. He'd expected that.

"Is it weird that this tastes good?" Glitch tossed an empty potion bottle into the air and watched it slowly dissolve. "It isn't liquid. It's pixels. We eat and drink *in a digital world.*"

"It's not *weird*," said a girl's snooty voice. "It's a foundational law of virtualization!"

Connor's classmate, Lisa Q., wasn't even looking at them. She had her nose in a Vid-Screen, a sort of floating tablet, and was expertly tapping the screen as she passed.

"The Pfluter Principle *clearly* states," she began to lecture.

But what the Pfluter Principle stated, Connor never found out. There was an almighty BANG! as one of the classroom doors burst apart. Chunks of wood and glass skittered across the floor. The pieces dissolved as they rolled while, behind them, a slobbering creature with blazing red eyes gave a "RAWWWRR!"

Connor's heart shook.

It was a monster.

A high-level monster!

2

RANKER

DROPS OF SPIT FELL LIKE RAIN FROM THE monster's jaws. It flew forward, its blazing eyes fixed on Connor.

My sword! Connor thought.

His hand twitched toward his Vid-Glove, then stopped.

The Wolf Buster Sword was *new*. He hadn't used it in battle yet. Could he even wield it? What if he messed up?

"Stay back, kids! That's not a fiend you can handle!"

Mr. Oldentone, the school janitor, came hopping out of the classroom. He aimed a silver broom at the monster. Its long bristles shimmered like icicles.

The fiend uttered a wail. It turned to flee, releasing a thick spray of slime to cover its tracks.

Half the lockers got drenched. So did Glitch's swim-goggle glasses. And *all* of Lisa.

"How in Suu's name do they keep getting *in?*" Mr. Oldentone grumbled. He raised his broom and gave chase. But not before he flipped Connor a token.

"You mind cleaning this up, son?"

Mr. Oldentone sped off.

Connor stared at the token.

"Hurry and smash it," said Glitch, wiping slime from his goggles.

Lisa's pink shirt was soaked. She didn't seem to mind, however. She tapped her Vid-Screen and yawned.

Weird, Connor thought.

He smashed the token. A wisp of smoke lifted into the air, along with a message:

CLEANING SPIRIT, LVL 3
Type: Minion
Skills: Purify, Lvl 3; Scour, Lvl 1
Duration: 60s

The Cleaning Spirit had green eyes and a swirling mouth. It hovered between the smashed door and lockers, its mouth pulling up slime like a vacuum cleaner.

"Could you maybe clean *her* first?" said Connor. He pointed to Lisa's slime-covered avatar.

The Cleaning Spirit sniffed haughtily.

"This is Level 5 Spectral Ooze," it said. "How could removing it be that simple? I can clean the hallway, but your friend will need to soak in the waters of Lake Blessed for at least one hour in order to just barely — HOW DID YOU DO THAT?"

The Cleaning Spirit stared in amazement. The slime on Lisa's skin and clothes had disappeared. Somehow, she'd even changed outfits.

These were not skills that an ordinary student should possess!

"Did you obtain a rare Witch's Wand, by chance? Are you a *Ranker*?"

The Cleaning Spirit peered into Lisa's eyes. As a summoned creature, however, it could only appear for short intervals. Just then, its timer expired.

It dissolved.

Lisa was still tapping her Vid-Screen. "Time to go," she told Connor. "Coming? We have ten minutes and a ten-minute walk."

Connor and Glitch traded looks.

"Are you really a Ranker?" Glitch blurted out.

"Don't be silly," said Lisa. "There are no fourth-grade Rankers. Do I look like I'm in middle school?"

She smiled innocently.

Connor's eyes narrowed. With a wave, he conjured a Vid-Screen of his own. A list of VGL's highest-ranked students beamed in front of him. He thumbed across it. None of the names were younger than twelve.

Glitch was even more baffled than Connor.

"If you're not a Ranker, then how did you—?" he started to say.

But Lisa was already gone.

3
VIDEO GAME ELEMENTARY

EXCEPT FOR TELEPORTATION, THE shortest route to Connor's classroom was through the Armorer's Tent, which was a brief walk from Main Hall, where their avatars spawned every morning.

Connor and Glitch used a side door to exit Main Hall and cross the busy VGL campus.

A minute later, they reached the Armorer's Tent.

It was BURNING.

Plumes of smoke drifted over the helmets and shields on display.

"Lava leak," said the armorer. "You'll want Level 5 boots if you come any closer."

Connor and Glitch slid to a halt behind a group of worried-looking fifth-graders. Even for them, obtaining Level 5 gear was no joke.

"Guess we're taking a detour," they sighed.

"Man, Oldentone must be slacking!"

They shuffled off.

In the VGL world, accidents such as leaking lava were common. They were also ANNOYING. Especially if you were running late to first period because you spent too long drinking Double-Up Potions in front of your respawn.

"So much for the shortcut," said Glitch. "These shields aren't too bad, though." He touched a shining red one. It hissed and turned a fuzzy maroon. The armorer shot him a look.

"We're leaving!" piped Connor.

The boys backtracked until they reached a bubbling stone fountain. Jets of water shot between the mouths of snarling statues with giant hooked claws.

"Fiend Fountain," said the signpost.

It was time to part ways.

In a cruel twist, Connor and Glitch had been assigned different teachers this year. Glitch's fourth-grade classroom was nowhere near Connor's. They wouldn't meet again until lunch.

"See you after school?" Glitch said hopefully. "We can hunt mobs in Gage Woods. I'm sure I can get my Vid-Glove under control. I just need more—"

"Can't," said Connor. "I've got Swords Team after class. My first practice."

He tried to keep the excitement from his voice. It wasn't easy. Swords Team was almost the only thing on his mind. He couldn't wait till school ended!

"Oh. Right." Glitch stared at his Vid-Glove. "Must be nice," he said gloomily.

With his busted Vid-Glove, Glitch couldn't play after-school sports. Even the simple ones used Vid-Glove abilities.

"Could you hold a sword in your normal hand?" Connor asked.

Glitch shook his head. "Not that easy. You saw the shield I touched. Anyway, I should go. It's a short walk, but *some of us* have books to carry."

Glitch's bookbag bounced in the air as he left. Of all the kids at VGL, only Glitch had to equip a separate storage item.

Connor sighed. He wanted to help Glitch. But how? Even *teachers* seemed confused by the situation.

The Vid-Glove was a virtual item.

It shouldn't malfunction, right?

Connor was frowning as he departed Fiend Fountain. He felt bad for upsetting Glitch. But as he began his own, longer walk to class, turning down the hill toward Lake Blessed, his mood lifted.

He drew an item out of storage.

RUSTY SLED, LVL 1
Type: Mobility
Rarity: E
Durability: D
Awesomeness: A++

The last rank was a custom note Connor added.

But it wasn't wrong.

Wind whipped at Connor's cheeks. He was sledding downhill, gaining speed. Perhaps not *as much* speed as he would've liked, but a slow sled was still totally cool!

He zoomed past Gage Woods, with its short trees and low-level mobs. He crossed the footpath and sped between large, jagged rocks.

Wherever he looked, he saw student avatars. Most were headed to class. Others held axes and spades, mining last-minute minerals, or slashed the air with bright weapons.

Connor gave a whoop as he passed them.

He felt heroic. Invincible!

It was amazing to think his real body was still at home, strapped into some whirring machine. "Full Immersion," the VR rig had advertised.

And the ad had been right!

Cruising downhill on the sled, he had never felt such incredible—

"Waahh!"

Connor screamed as the Lake Blessed waters erupted. A towering fiend broke the surface, showing a single bright eye the size of a minivan.

Although the eye didn't move, Connor did. He veered sideways, grabbing even more speed. The sled began to creak. Connor swerved again, hit a bump and went flying off the sled and into the air.

He landed hard on his feet.

Down below, the empty sled hit a rock.

It exploded.

"Worth it," said Connor as the sled vanished from his inventory. He walked the rest of the way with a big grin on his face.

The VGL world was totally awesome!

Technically, VGL stood for VIRTUAL GUIDED LEARNING. But to the kids in Connor's class, and to anyone lucky enough to attend a VGL school of their own, the letters meant something else.

VIDEO GAME ELEMENTARY ("VGL")

The acronym wasn't perfect. If you said it aloud, it just barely made sense. Which was a good way to describe the VGL world. It was a mish-mash of gaming elements. Its creator, Atensoft, Inc., had even based the school on a video game it was working on.

They were always making updates.

Every day brought more killer features.

New regions. Improved crafting and battle systems. Even an increased risk of death! (Although you didn't *die*; your avatar just respawned in Detention).

Connor's smile grew wide. He reached the school building without really thinking. Only later, crossing the spinning glass entrance, did he finally remember where he was headed.

His smile faded.

Ms. Vickers's fourth-grade classroom.

As he reached the drab yellow door, a voice was already shouting, "You're late!"

4
TOTAL SNOOZEFEST

CONNOR SCURRIED INTO THE CLASSROOM.

He ducked a spinning art mobile, then skirted a wall of boring math charts and "Capitals of the World" posters. There was even a picture: two kids with stiff-looking smiles, each holding books and exchanging an awkward high-five.

Those poor kids, Connor thought.

He flopped into the chair next to Lisa. She had a large notebook and several pens on her desk, and a small Vid-Screen across her lap. She was typing in secret while beaming up at Ms. Vickers, who was scratching "CONNOR LAMB" in block letters across her old-fashioned blackboard.

SCRITCH. SCRITCH. SCRITCH.

The awful sound made Connor's skin crawl.

"Strike one, Connor," Ms. Vickers announced.

Connor leaned across Lisa's desk.

"How did you get here so fast?" he whispered.

Lisa smirked at him. "Shortcut."

• • • • • • • • • •

"WELCOME TO A NEW WEEK OF LEARNING!"

Ms. Vickers strode forward. Her avatar was a short, white-haired woman in a dress stamped with tulips.

"Since we last met, I have removed Self Defense and Visual Math from our schedule. My aim, as you know, is to *minimize* your use of Vid-Gloves. Call me old-fashioned, but as your teacher, I hope to provide a more *traditional* — Mr. Lamb, eyes on me, please."

Connor jumped in his chair.

"I assure you, the clock on my wall will not move any faster with you staring at it," said Ms. Vickers.

Connor's face reddened. He also drew in his arm, which had been practicing Swords Team techniques in the aisle.

"Moving on," said Ms. Vickers.

But she was soon interrupted.

BOOOM! A massive noise shook the hallway.

"Fiend? Is that a fiend?" shouted everyone.

The floor quaked. The desks wobbled. Posters fell like rain from the shivering corkboards. ("Sometimes Later Becomes Never," one advised. "Do it Now!")

Ms. Vickers slammed the classroom door. "That's *it*!" she cried. "I've had enough of this. More than enough!"

She grabbed an empty chair and wedged it under the door knob, forming a barricade.

"Monsters!" she huffed. "Fiends in the hallways!" She drew a shuddering breath.

"Now, I am grateful for what the Atensoft corporation has given us. Truly, I am. But why such remarkable software must include *VIDEO GAME ELEMENTS*—" Ms. Vickers's voice rose in annoyance, "I shall never know. If it were up to me, I would delete every sword, every fiend, every trading tent!"

Her tiny arms shook.

"Alas, I cannot. Nor will I sit idly by as my class is disrupted by nonsense. This is a hall of learning, not a battlefield! The time has come, I'm afraid. We must fight fire with fire."

Ms. Vickers pulled up her dress sleeve. She tapped the rather large Vid-Glove beneath it. There was an ominous sound.

"Ow!" Connor yelped. He felt a squeezing sensation. Other kids were moaning and tapping their arms.

Nothing worked.

Every Vid-Glove in the room had shut down!

Ms. Vickers smiled smugly. "No Internet searches, no calculators," she recited. "From now until the final bell, there will be no apps allowed in my classroom. If I see even a hint of a *video game*—" her voice stiffened, "it's full detention. Understood?"

Connor gaped at her. So did everyone.

"I can't *hear* you," sang Ms. Vickers.

"Yes, Ms. Vickers," the class mumbled.

"Excellent. Now pencils out. I'd like to begin with a handwritten essay ..."

"EIGHT FORTY TWO ..."

"*Still* eight forty two ..."

"Eight forty two *again*? Seriously?"

Connor scowled at the wall clock. A whole seven minutes had passed.

It felt like ninety nine hours.

His wrist ached from his handwriting. He wasn't used to holding pencils in the VGL world. Feeling bitter, Connor turned his essay into a story about a teacher abducted by aliens. It was a funny story. But it didn't make the clock turn any faster.

At nine twenty five, Ms. Vickers made everyone recite a poem out of a thick book.

At ten ten, with Connor in full zombie mode, they watched a slideshow on the water cycle. *Condensation. Transpiration. Precipitation.* The words banged around in Connor's head, causing +5 psychic damage.

Probably.

With his Vid-Glove turned off, he couldn't read his own health bar.

Finally, the lunch bell sounded. Connor checked his skin for old age spots. Finding none, he rushed to the teleporter. He couldn't wait to see Glitch.

But back at Main Hall, where all the fourth-graders teleported, Glitch's avatar was missing. Connor looked everywhere, including inside the Potions Machine.

Where is he? Detention? Connor wondered.

At recess, Connor and his class stood and watched as everyone else raced around. They played Virtual Kart and split their loot crates with giant claw hammers.

"Can we *please* have our Vid-Gloves back?" Connor begged.

"Three o'clock," said Ms. Vickers. "Not a moment sooner."

Twelve thirty.

One o'clock.

One fifteen.

Was time slowing down or was long division warping his mind? Connor didn't know the answer to that, or to any of his quiz questions. It felt like a hamburger had replaced his brain. He was still trying and failing to use it when a light flickered.

His eyes swiveled. *Lisa.*

A Vid-Screen glowed in her lap. She was typing!

"Hey! How are you doing that?" Connor hissed.

Everyone knew that Vid-Screens were summoned by Vid-Gloves. You couldn't use one without the other. So how was she doing it?

"Doing what?" Lisa said innocently.

She waved the Vid-Screen away, just as Ms. Vickers marched up the aisle. Connor sighed. He returned to his math quiz.

Time ticked on.

Two o'clock was a turning point. Connor felt his heart stirring. He stopped trying to get Lisa's attention and started rubbing his arm. He could almost feel his Vid-Glove booting up again.

Two fifty five.

Two fifty eight.

Two fifty *nine.*

The second hand sped toward the finish. Connor watched with bated breath. His knees bounced like crazy.

Two seconds.

One second.

But on the last tick, something happened. There was a loud hiss, as if Glitch had interfered somehow.

Then a bleep.

Then a staticky *crack*.

A moment later, the VGL world turned to white.

5

TRAPPED IN CLASS

SCRITCH. SCRITCH. SCRITCH.

Ms. Vickers was writing the name "CONNOR LAMB" in block letters across her old-fashioned blackboard.

Connor rubbed his eyes.

His first thought was, *What kind of maniac puts a realistic blackboard scratch sound in a video game?*

His second thought, peering up at the blackboard, was, *Wait, haven't I seen this before?*

"Strike one, Connor," Ms. Vickers announced.

Connor peered at the clock.

"No way," he whispered.

All around him, kids were tapping their Vid-Gloves. Pencils and notebooks appeared on their desks with small pops.

"I'm bored already," someone yawned.

"First period is worst period," a voice agreed.

Connor leaned across Lisa's desk. "Uh, this might sound weird but — what day is it?"

Lisa put a finger to her lips. "Shhh!"

She went back to typing.

Connor slumped at his desk. He eyed the clock again.

"Eight thirty five?" he muttered. "Eight thirty five *in the morning?*"

Was that even possible?

"Mr. Lamb, eyes on me, please."

Connor jumped in his chair.

"I assure you, the clock on my wall will not move any faster with you staring at it," said Ms. Vickers.

"You said that last time," Connor blurted out.

Ms. Vickers locked eyes with him. "I do not appreciate your tone, young man."

Connor couldn't believe it.

"But … you did!" he cried. "All of this—" he waved dramatically, "it already happened. I lived it! I was here in class until three o'clock. Then I don't know, something went wrong. This huge glitch. And the school day restarted!"

"Would you like a second strike, Connor?"

"I'm telling the truth! You have to believe me!"

"That's it, you're getting an underline!"

Ms. Vickers stormed to the blackboard. She had just raised her chalk to Connor's name when—

BOOOM! A massive noise shook the hallway.

Ms. Vickers let out a shriek. Forgetting all about Connor's strike, she slammed the classroom door, then launched into a furious rant about *video game elements*.

A minute later, there was an ominous sound.

Every Vid-Glove in the room powered off.

· · · ● · ● ● · · ·

"PRECIPITATION ... TRANSPORTATION ... Perspiration? Wait, no—"

Connor's voice stumbled. Ms. Vickers was shaking her head.

"Incorrect. *Wildly* incorrect. Goodness! I don't know what's gotten into you today, Connor."

The day is REPEATING, thought Connor. *That's what's gotten into me!*

But he didn't dare say it out loud.

After almost getting an underline, which was a circle away from detention, he'd decided not to stand up and yell.

But he was still on the case.

"Psst! I think we're trapped in a time loop," Connor whispered.

"Yeah, sure," said his classmates. "Whatever."

Even Lisa, who was normally friendly, kept shushing him.

Lisa never shushed him!

Okay, she *sometimes* did. But seven times in a row?

"I'll prove it," said Connor. But after predicting the items in all seven loot crates at recess, kids just laughed and said, "Lucky guess."

Connor was fuming.

He wished his Flux account wasn't linked to his Vid-Glove. (Flux was VGL's in-game currency). Otherwise he could've won some big bets.

But would winning a bet even matter?

That was the real question.

At three o'clock, would Connor cruise through the door on his way to Swords Team practice? Or would the day loop again, erasing all that had happened?

Connor spent the afternoon crossing his fingers.

And crossing his feet.

And wiping sweat off his avatar's forehead.

Everything will be fine, he told himself. *Last time I hit some weird bug. The game probably crashed. It sent me back to a checkpoint.*

Connor nodded to himself.

He liked this idea very much.

Video games crashed all the time. But not *every* time. It was almost impossible to trigger the same bug in the same exact way.

Right?

And even if it *could* trigger twice, Atensoft's programmers were geniuses. They would've *definitely* found the bug and patched it already.

Right?

Right?

As a student avatar, Connor couldn't just "disconnect" from the VGL world. He had to wait for the school day to finish. But what if his

Monday class *never* finished? What if it went on repeating forever?

Connor shivered in his chair. He looked around at his classmates. They suddenly seemed different.

Not like kids anymore.

More like NPCs.

Non-player characters.

A light flickered. Connor turned and saw Lisa's mysterious, impossible Vid-Screen.

Lisa's eyes were scrunched up. She was typing furiously.

Two fifty nine, said the clock.

Connor's eyes tracked the skinny second hand. He felt jittery like a jackrabbit, and nearly exploded out of his seat when Lisa's hand touched him.

"See you on Monday," she said with a wink.

Connor's brain did a somersault. He opened his mouth. But before he could speak, something hissed!

Something bleeped!

Something crackled with static!

The VGL world turned to white.

6
THE THIRD STRIKE

SCRITCH. SCRITCH. SCRITCH.

It was that sound again!

Connor's skin crawled. He peered at the clock. Eight thirty five, it said, as a familiar name appeared on the old-fashioned blackboard.

"CONNOR LAMB."

The block letters leered at him.

He didn't care.

He leaned across Lisa's desk.

"You did something!" he hissed. "Fess up! What did you do to me?"

"Shh!" Lisa said. "It wasn't me, okay? Just hold on."

With a tap, she summoned a new, larger Vid-Screen. It hovered over her desk, in plain view of everyone.

Lisa's fingers danced in the air.

"Come on," she begged. "Come on!"

Ms. Vickers, who was about to say, "Strike one, Connor," almost shrieked in alarm. A Vid-Screen? In *her* classroom?

"Miss Q!" she cried. "What is the meaning of this?"

Lisa didn't react. She kept typing.

Ms. Vickers shuddered with anger. She whirled to the blackboard. A second later, the name "LISA Q." appeared in block letters next to Connor's.

A second after *that*, it was underlined.

"*Lisa*," Connor warned.

But his voice struck a nerve. Now Ms. Vickers turned and gave HIM an underline.

Connor gasped.

At the same time, Lisa jumped to her feet. Ignoring the shocked looks of everyone, she cried, "I did it! IT WORKED!"

"Return to your seat!" Ms. Vickers demanded.

"No thanks." Lisa beamed at their teacher.

Then she reached out and clamped Connor's wrist! Connor felt a stab of horror as Lisa dragged him into the aisle beside her.

"We have work to do," Lisa announced. "Right, Connor?"

There were gasps. Even Ms. Vickers gave a small shriek. She tugged her tulip-stamped dress, looking shell-shocked.

"I don't know *what* is going on today," she declared, "but I certainly know how to handle it. The Principal's Office. Both of you!"

Ms. Vickers raised her chalk to the blackboard. She circled their underlined names.

"*Finally*," Lisa whispered.

The block letters trembled. Beams of light burst from the blackboard, which had become a swirling vortex. The beams shot up the aisle like glowing ropes, wrapping Connor and Lisa in sparkling cocoons.

Connor felt a tingling sensation.

His avatar lifted into the air.

A moment later, he was sucked through the blackboard.

7
LISA'S SECRET

THE VGL WORLD BECAME A SWIRLING black blur. Connor's avatar twisted and turned. His heart raced. Then came a rushing sound. The turns stopped.

He was FALLING.

"Waaaah!" Connor yelled.

Acting on instinct, he swiveled his hips (he had a knack for tricky maneuvers) and when the floor arrived, he landed neatly on both feet.

BOOOM!

Lisa's avatar crashed beside him. She crumpled to the floor and lay still, emitting puffs of thin smoke.

"Uh, Lisa? You alive in there?"

"Critically Low Health!" said a message.

Lisa groaned and sat up. "Overshot the landing a bit, didn't I? But other than that—" she peered around at the lockers, "*It worked.* I knew it would work, and it did!"

Lisa beamed as she climbed to her feet. She used five Flux to buy a Double-Up Potion at the nearby machine. As her health bar refilled, Connor finally forced some answers out of her.

Yes, Lisa knew about the time loop.

No, she didn't *cause* it. At least, she swore she didn't.

"I just didn't panic like *you* did," said Lisa. "I find it fascinating. A stable time loop. A day that keeps repeating forever. Do you know how much stuff we could learn if we stayed inside the loop and just *studied*? But I suppose there's a risk we'd forget it all coming out. Pfluter's Third Law, you know."

"Sure," Connor mumbled.

Fortunately, the second part of Lisa's story was more encouraging.

"I've been trying to break the loop," Lisa said. "During our last restart I kept quiet on purpose. I'm good at programming, so I decided to track the VGL game code in real time. I was scanning for bugs. You almost messed me up, by the way. All your interrupting. If you just learned to relax more—"

"Relax?" Connor snorted. "*You* were the crazy one! You talked back to Ms. Vickers! You got us black-holed to Principal Norris's—"

Connor paused as he became aware of his surroundings. The high table. The long rows of lockers. The familiar-looking Potions Machine with a dent where a glitched Vid-Glove slapped it.

"We're back in *Main Hall?*" Connor gasped.

Lisa grinned at him.

"I hacked Ms. Vickers's teleporter. At first, I wasn't sure you *could* hack them. But whoever wrote that part of VGL's game code was sloppy. Anyway, I figured us getting three strikes was the smartest way to skip class. Ms. Vickers won't be expecting us back any time soon. Besides, it's not like we haven't done the work twice already. What?"

Connor was shaking his head.

"You have cheat codes — *for the VGL world*?"

"A few." Lisa laughed. "Now come on, I didn't jump us back to Main Hall by chance." She summoned a Vid-Screen. "I'm getting strange readings from these lockers. Whatever caused the loop, I think it started right here."

Connor mulled it over. "We were both at Main Hall this morning," he said slowly. "That can't be coincidence. But then what about Glitch? He was here. Mr. Oldentone, too. And that creature, that—"

"*Fiend*," Lisa whispered.

"Yeah, that. Massive jaws. Blazing eyes. Not to mention the foul-smelling — uh, Lisa? Why does your face look so—?"

"FIEND!" shouted Lisa. "BEHIND YOU!"

8
THE WOLF BUSTER SWORD

DROPS OF SPIT FELL LIKE RAIN FROM THE monster's jaws. It flew forward, its blazing eyes fixed on Connor. *Again.*

Connor's heart quaked. He didn't know which was more shocking, the fiend or Lisa's sudden reaction. Normally calm, her avatar fell to the floor, shaking fearfully.

"What happened to 'You need to relax more?'" Connor hissed.

Lisa uttered a wail.

"I'm useless in battle," she moaned. "I can't type under pressure. I can't think. I can't *move.*"

She clutched Connor's ankles.

"Connor, please! My avatar is squishy. I'm low-leveled! If I take even one direct hit—"

At that moment, the fiend let loose with a "RAWWR!" that sent locker doors flying open. It hopped forward, showing fangs wet with slime.

"Do something!" Lisa begged.

The fiend's stats appeared in a floating text box.

FANGED SLIME, LVL 2
Type: Gelatinous
Power: C
Speed: C
Defense: E

Level 2? Connor's throat tightened. Though it wasn't Level 5, like the fiend Mr. Oldentone chased, this Fanged Slime was still a nasty opponent. Its C-rank Power and Speed would push Connor's skills to the limit.

Levels in the VGL world were no joke. What with starting classes last month, then trying to hunt down a weapon, Connor had barely managed to—

"Oh!" His mind stopped.

A *weapon!*

Connor pounded his Vid-Glove. His stomach swirled as the sword beamed to life. It was long and heavy, with a stain on its hilt.

WOLF BUSTER SWORD
Type: Melee Weapon
Rarity: C
Durability: E

Additional Information: The bane of the wolf! Grants +5 Attack against Wolf-type fiends. Brittle. Unsuited for everyday use.

Connor had never thought of himself as a hero. In real life, he was the furthest thing from a hero that ever existed. Ask anyone at his old, offline school. You'd get the same howl of laughter.

Connor Lamb? *Hero?*

The kid who ate lunch at his locker?

The guy who fainted when his thumb started bleeding?

But here in the VGL world, with a mighty sword in his grasp, and Lisa Q. crouched behind him, afraid for her life, Connor felt a rush of adrenaline — a surge of fighting spirit he never knew he possessed.

Wind whipped at his ears.

He rushed forward.

"Attaaaackk!" Connor cried.

9
VICTORY AND DEFEAT

ATTAAAACKK? CONNOR THOUGHT.

As battle cries went, it was pretty lame. He'd have to work on it.

FWOOSH. The Wolf Buster Sword wobbled over his head.

Heavy, heavy, heavy.

Connor gritted his teeth. He growled and gave a last effort. The sword teetered. Slowly at first, and then almost too quickly, it tipped toward the fiend's bulbous body. So did Connor. He couldn't bear the huge weight!

KA-CHING!

The sword showed its might, slicing the Fanged Slime in two.

SPLAT!

Connor faceplanted, *hard*, in the goopy remains. There were loud slurps as he struggled for balance. The Fanged Slime was reforming. Pools of goop crawled together, forming quivering mounds.

Connor panicked. Unable to stand, he dropped the Wolf Buster Sword and rolled onto his back, then onto his front, then onto his back again.

SPLAT! SPLAT! SPLAT!

The mounds suffered hit after hit. Finally, they sank and collapsed.

A message floated into the air.

ENEMY DEFEATED!
FANGED SLIME, LVL 2
+ 22 XP, + 5 Flux
Drops: None

Streams of XP and Flux flooded into Connor's Vid-Glove. He gave a wild whoop. No, he hadn't leveled up. He hadn't snagged an item drop, either.

But who cared? He had done it. He'd solo-killed his first fiend!

"This sword *rocks!*" Connor whooped again.

Behind him, Lisa bounced to her feet.

"First of all," she said snootily, "you can barely *lift* a sword with your measly Strength stat. Second, you almost died to *a Level 2 Slime.* You got lucky. If you hadn't tripped and rolled over—"

"Are you kidding me?" said Connor. "I saved your butt just now. You were totally panicked!"

"*You* were panicked," said Lisa. "I was just surprised. With enough warning, I could beat *twenty* Fanged Slimes like yours. Easy."

Connor rolled his eyes.

He raised his Wolf Buster Sword again. It didn't feel heavy at all! Although he hadn't learned many moves, he did a quick combo just to prove Lisa wrong.

His sword moved like lightning. Slash. Slash again. Only on the last move (a slash) did he notice his missing sword tip.

"WHAT!" Connor yelled.

The heavy blade was dissolving.

Lisa almost fainted with laughter. "You used *a Wolf Buster Sword* on a Slime fiend? Their slime is toxic! It can eat through most Sword types."

Connor's face paled. "Save my sword!" he begged. "Use your cheat codes!"

But even as he spoke, the last piece of hilt turned to mist. The Wolf Buster Sword vanished from Connor's inventory.

"This is why Melee fighting is lame," said Lisa. "Boys think they can just swing a sword and kill anything. Ridiculous. Ranged attacks are much smarter."

"Says the girl who was helpless a minute ago!"

"You're exaggerating," said Lisa.

"You're delusional!" Connor shot back.

He couldn't believe her behavior. It was one thing to reprogram the VGL game code. But you couldn't reprogram the truth. How could life be that easy?

Lisa summoned a Vid-Screen. "The fiend didn't appear by accident," she said, switching topics. "We're lucky it was just a wimpy Slime-type—"

"Delusional," Connor repeated.

"—because a reading this weird could draw anything."

Lisa tapped her Vid-Screen and started to walk.

"Fiends sniff out changes in VGL's code," she explained. "Normally it means a new dungeon was added, or a rare item. Fiends love that stuff. Apparently a weird bug has an equal attraction. Yep, just as I suspected!"

Lisa pointed to a closed classroom door.

"CUSTODIAN'S OFFICE 8A," it said. "CUSTODIANS ONLY."

"Isn't that the door that exploded?" said Connor. "Huh. It almost looks new again. I wonder if that Level 3 Cleaning Spirit—?"

"Important doors fix *themselves*," Lisa lectured. "They don't need Cleaning Spirits."

"Know-it-all," Connor muttered.

Lisa's eyes were glued to her Vid-Screen.

"The weirdness is coming from inside this office," she said. "I guarantee it. The code never lies."

She opened the door without looking.

WHOOSH. In the open doorway, a clump of pixels suddenly swelled like balloons. They wobbled and flashed a dull gray.

"Lisa, look out! Something's wrong!" Connor warned.

Lisa *still* didn't look. She strode forward with her nose in a Vid-Screen.

"I read game code the way you see with your eyes," she bragged. "Better, actually. My Vid-Screen gives me all the vision I—"

FWOOP.

Lisa's avatar stiffened.

Time stopped.

10
GLITCH

LISA FLOATED IN THE OPEN DOORWAY.
She looked frozen in time, as if someone had
pressed "Pause" on her avatar.

Not Pause, Connor realized. *Slow motion.*

Extremely slow motion.

After a full minute, Lisa's head had turned half
an inch. The weird pixels seemed to restrict the
flow of time somehow.

Connor frowned. First a time loop, and now a
time ultra-slowdown? It was definitely fishy. He
felt a rush of longing. He wanted more than ever
to see inside of that office.

But how could he?

How could anyone cross those weird pixels?

Connor tapped his Vid-Glove. His first goal was to rescue Lisa. Would a Haste Rune help? What about an Escape Rope? In the end, it hardly mattered. He found neither item in his inventory.

"5x iron ore," he read aloud. "*6x pebble*? That's useless!"

He had summoned the pebbles, just to chuck them into the time field, when his Vid-Glove made an ominous sound.

"No, no, no!" Connor cried as his Vid-Glove unpowered. "I don't *believe* it. Ms. Vickers switched them off again. Of course she did. Stupid time loop!"

"Gggggggggg—" said Lisa's avatar.

Connor looked up. Lisa's head had turned sideways to face him. Her lips moved at the speed of molasses.

"Gggggggggg—" she went on.

A full minute passed.

"Ooooooooooo," she said.

"Go?" Connor blinked at her. "Go where? And do what?"

He couldn't think of an item to find. And anyway, how could he farm drops without a sword? Without a *Vid-Glove*?

In theory, a teacher could help. Teachers had powerful avatars. In practice, however, most teachers were dreadful gamers. They couldn't solve a problem like this.

So *how can* I? Connor thought miserably.

He stared at Lisa's avatar. She looked like a bug in a web. A slow-motion bug in a slow-motion web.

Beside her, the messed-up pixels were glowing. They hissed and shook and changed colors.

Definitely a glitch, Connor thought.

His heart jolted. Glitch!

· · · ● ● · ● ● · · ·

THE ARMORER'S TENT WAS no longer burning when Connor pushed through the flap. He raced toward the shortcut.

"Hold it right there!" said a voice.

Connor slid to a halt. Well, he meant to.

"Whoaa!"

His shoes slipped on ice. A heavy arm hooked his waist before he skidded too far. It belonged to the armorer.

"Strange weather," he drawled. "First it burned. Now it's freezing. Server's a right mess today. But one fact remains: you'll need proper equipment to cross the shortcut. For instance—"

"Level 5 boots," Connor muttered.

"Aye. Might be a sled would do, if you risk it."

A *sled!*

Connor groaned. His luck was really too poor today.

On his way out, he passed the armorer's junk heap. He did a double take. The shield Glitch had touched lay on top. Tufts of fur sprouted over the metal. Apparently the shield was no longer fit for sale and could only be scrapped.

The armorer caught Connor eyeing it. He clearly put two and two together, because he started to yell.

"Oy! You there!"

Connor bolted.

IN THE END, IT took Connor twice as long to backtrack to Fiend Fountain and cross the spinning glass entrance to Glitch's school building.

The building was identical to Connor's, so he had no trouble finding Glitch's classroom. If anything, he found it too quickly.

"Uh, Glitch? Is Glitch here?" Connor blurted out.

He froze in the open doorway, feeling rather like Lisa, as Glitch's fourth-grade teacher, Mr. Lively, stared down his glasses and turned from the blackboard.

"*Sven*," he said stiffly, "is tardy. Who are you? Why are you roaming my hallway?"

Connor flushed. "Uh … bathroom break?"

As soon as he said it, he cringed.

"There are no bathrooms at VGL," Mr. Lively intoned. "It is, perhaps, the most famous exception to Pfluter's Seventh Conjecture—"

Pfluter! Connor uttered a moan.

"So I ask again, young man: why are you roaming my hallway?"

Connor had no answer to that. He made a funny gurgling noise with his throat. Then he turned heel and ran.

His footsteps echoed in the empty hallway. Was he being chased? Would Mr. Lively come sprinting after him?

Connor didn't pause to look back. But he *did* pause. He stopped dead as a voice rang out:

"Help! Help!"

One of the lockers was shaking. Connor pressed his ear to it.

"Glitch?" he said.

"Connor? That you?"

Connor opened the locker. Glitch was indeed crammed inside. His swim-goggle glasses hung sideways and his bookbag had clipped through a wall. He was stuck worse than Lisa!

With a mighty pull, Connor dragged Glitch into the hallway.

"Thanks," said Glitch. "I owe you one."

"What happened?" said Connor.

"Nothing," Glitch mumbled.

But Connor asked again, and Glitch finally came out with it.

"Some kids shut me into my locker," said Glitch. "It's fine. I'm used to it. I don't mind being called 'Defect' or 'Bookbag Boy,' either. But today, for some reason, my bookbag got stuck."

"It's *not* fine," said Connor. "This happens to you a lot? Some dorks shut you into your locker?"

Glitch shrugged. "I can usually slip out."

Connor scowled. Who knew Glitch's classmates were such bullies? To Connor, Glitch was cool. His messed-up avatar was exciting and full of surprises.

Unfortunately, Glitch didn't see it that way. And why would he? It was Glitch, not Connor, who had to live every day with a busted Vid-Glove. He wore a bookbag item kids laughed at. He couldn't play after-school sports …

There was a long silence.

"I should get to class," Glitch said finally.

"Why? Haven't you been twice already?"

"Huh?" Glitch stared through his swim goggles.

The truth dawned on Connor.

"You aren't part of the time loop," he said slowly. "You have no idea what I'm talking about."

"I'm definitely out of the loop on this one," said Glitch. "Are you sure you're feeling okay? Did you fight a Brain-Eating Bat on your way to class?"

Connor laughed. He grabbed Glitch and steered him toward the exit.

He told him everything.

11

THE TIME FIELD

"NO," SAID GLITCH. "NUH-UH. NO WAY."

"Yes way," said Connor, again and again.

It was no use. Glitch refused to believe him.

"If you're *really* trapped in a time loop," said Glitch, "then prove it. Tell the future."

He pointed to a red-haired girl crossing Fiend Fountain ahead of them.

"Which way does she turn? Left or right?"

"How should I know?" said Connor. "I wasn't here when she—"

"How about him?" said Glitch. "Or him? Or those kids over there?"

Glitch hopped around, pointing at random.

"Come on!" he said. "You're a time traveler, right? You should know things!"

• • • • ● • ● • • •

THOUGH SHORT, THE WALK to Main Hall was exhausting. Glitch had a million demands. He wanted proof that the time loop existed. It didn't matter how many times Connor explained that he'd only lived the day twice, spending both loops in Ms. Vickers's classroom.

"What about recess?" said Glitch. "Hey, yeah! What did I do?"

"No idea," said Connor. "You weren't there. You weren't at lunch, either."

"What!" cried Glitch. "You mean I never got out of my locker? Those *dorks!*"

"Dorks," Connor agreed. "Next time we're in a PvP zone, we are totally trashing them."

"I don't know," said Glitch. "They're pretty tanky. One of them even does Swords Team," he added gloomily.

"Oh," Connor said with a frown.

FORTUNATELY, GLITCH'S GLOOMY MOOD didn't last. It vanished as soon as he saw Lisa.

"Hey Lisa, how's it going? Pretty slow? I'll bet it's slow. Is it slow?"

Glitch shook with laughter.

Lisa was indeed a funny sight. Her avatar floated in the open doorway. She moved at a snail's pace, almost frozen in time, although her expression had changed since Connor last saw it. It was now very clearly a scowl.

"Catch!" yelled a voice.

Connor turned and snagged the Double-Up Potion Glitch tossed him.

"You're lucky I have killer reflexes," said Connor.

"Cheers," said Glitch.

He left the Potions Machine, which was trembling again, and clinked his potion against the one he'd thrown Connor.

"To not being stuck!" said Glitch.

He winked at Lisa's avatar.

There was the tiniest twitch from her eyelid.

"Careful," Connor warned. "You don't want Lisa Q. for an enemy, trust me."

He told Glitch about her cheat codes.

"Scary." Glitch shuddered.

"Can you help her?" Connor asked.

"What? Pull her out of the time field?" Glitch shook his head. "I don't have powers like that. It's the opposite. Whatever I touch either blows up or gets randomly worse."

"Your power is glitching," said Connor.

He pointed at the time field.

"That's a glitch. Normal methods won't fix it. But what if we add *another* glitch? You know that old saying, 'Two wrongs make a right?'"

"I don't think that's a saying."

"We have to do *something*," said Connor. "I know you don't believe me, but the time loop is real. In a way, I'm just as trapped as Lisa right now."

Glitch was biting his lip.

"You just have to touch the doorway," said Connor. "Maybe nothing will happen. But if something does, it could free Lisa. It might even let us enter Mr. Oldentone's office. We think there are clues inside that could help us escape."

Glitch glanced from the time field to Connor.

"Oh all right," he said. "But I'm warning you, if I end up frozen in time next to Lisa Q. …"

Connor laughed. "So what if you do? It's a time loop. We can try again in six hours."

"So weird," Glitch mumbled.

He shut his eyes and stepped to the doorway. His Vid-Glove arm slowly stretched out. It brushed the time field and—

BOOOM!

12
COLLAPSE

"GLITCH! YOU OKAY, DUDE?"

Connor opened his eyes to find the time field still shaking. There were loud hisses. Strange bleeps. Even staticky cracks.

But loudest of all was a slurping sound.

FWOOP.

Glitch's avatar stiffened. He floated into the air, just as Lisa had. Instead of freezing, however, the time field around him *sped up*.

The air blurred. Glitch spun in dizzying loops.

But not Lisa. Her avatar emerged with a pop, stumbling into the hallway. Her face flashed with a million expressions. She hopped, skipped and wiggled her arms, reminding Connor of a cell phone unfreezing after you tapped every button.

Her voice was shrill like a chipmunk.

"Glitch-you-twerp-shut-your-mouth-Connor-you-too-if-I-ever-get-out-you-are-dead-I-will-hack-you-so-hard—"

"Slow down," said Connor.

"*Slow down?*" Lisa whirled on him. "Say that one more time. I dare you!"

"SLLLLOOOOOWWWW!" cried a boy's shaky voice. Or perhaps it was, "WHOOOOAAAAA!"

It was hard to tell *what* Glitch was screaming as the time field ejected him. He landed with a thump, then bread-rolled across the tile floor until he bounced off of Connor.

"It's over! It finally ended! I'm out!"

Glitch crawled to his knees.

"I-It was awful," he wheezed. "My vision blanked, then I woke up trapped in my locker. I was stuck there for *hours*. Then I heard these weird noises—"

"Like a hiss? Then a bleep? Then a staticky crack?" Connor asked.

"Exactly." Glitch shuddered. "That's when the day started over. I could tell because the dents I'd left in my locker disappeared. I thought I'd never get out. And I didn't at first. The day looped *again*."

Connor whistled. "Two and a half loops. I guess you caught up to Lisa and me. Talk about time compression. Out here only a few seconds passed." Connor grinned. "Do you believe me now?"

Glitch didn't speak. He was shaking too hard.

And suddenly, so was the time field.

The ripples from Glitch's exit had swelled into waves. There were deep rumbles. Messed-up pixels began spilling into the hallway, stacking up like toy blocks.

"Uh oh," said Connor.

The pixels bounced through the halls. They climbed lockers. They clicked and hissed as they jumped to the ceiling, replacing the VGL world with a jumble of weird, glitchy blocks.

Then came a BANG!

The time field collapsed.

13

SPACE FAIL

"WELL," SAID LISA, LOOKING UP FROM HER Vid-Screen, "at least the time field is gone. We can enter Mr. Oldentone's office now. Theoretically."

"Yeah. Great," Connor muttered.

In the aftermath of the explosion, Connor, Glitch and Lisa did a brief walking tour of Main Hall.

Very brief, in fact.

They completed the tour in ten steps.

The change was alarming. Spikes rose from the old tile floor. Triangles jutted from walls. The exploded blocks tangled and twisted together, forming ludicrous shapes.

Connor, Glitch and Lisa found themselves trapped on a small stretch of floor that resembled an island.

Everything else was the sea.

A sea that couldn't be crossed.

"The time slow turned into *a space fail?*" said Connor.

"Sorry," Glitch mumbled. "It's my fault. Nothing good comes from a glitch."

"You helped me escape the time field," said Lisa. "That was a good thing. Brave, too, considering I have backdoor access to VGL game code. *I heard you laughing,*" she whispered, with a flick of her Vid-Screen.

There was a *pop* and Glitch's goggles turned pink, sprouting fairy wings. Lisa beamed. But not for long. The goggles hissed as they returned to normal.

Glitch cackled. He pretended to blow smoke off his busted Vid-Glove.

"You're no fun," Lisa pouted.

Connor motioned Glitch over. While Lisa scanned the game code for bugs, the boys took turns launching themselves at Mr. Oldentone's doorway.

"Nope," Connor said. "Still can't reach it."

Glitch sighed with embarrassment.

It felt like the VGL software was trolling them. Either that, or they were actively cursed. During the blast, Mr. Oldentone's doorway had taken flight. Literally. It now hovered several feet over their heads.

Connor groaned as his jump missed again. "Anyone got a trampoline item? Pogo stick? Concussion grenade?"

"I can't hack the doorway code, either," said Lisa. "It's too buggy. I can tell Mr. Oldentone's office is safe to enter, but unless the doorway floats lower, we'll never reach it."

Glitch experimented with short jabs of his Vid-Glove. The doorway hissed and flew higher.

"Ow!" said Glitch. "Who threw that?"

"Bulls-eye," said Connor. He grinned as his second pebble bounced against Glitch's bookbag.

That's when something odd happened. The pebble bounced beneath the floating doorway, hit the air and bounced back.

Solid air?

Connor's eyes narrowed. He flung more pebbles, and soon discovered a pair of invisible walls supporting the doorway.

He stepped between them, placing his palms on both walls.

His eyes lit up.

"I've got an idea!" he announced.

· · · ● · ● · ● · ● · ·

"HOW CAN HE CLIMB that?" Lisa marveled. "I get that the walls are invisible, but they're *smooth.* There's nothing to grab onto!"

"Connor's like a ninja," said Glitch. "Plus his avatar has a Speed bonus."

"A Speed bonus?" Lisa frowned. "Then why would he carry a sword? That's a Strength weapon."

"Because swords are awesome? Duh." Glitch turned his gaze back to Connor, who was shimmying up a chute of invisible blocks.

"Boys," Lisa muttered.

One very long minute later, Connor collapsed in front of Mr. Oldentone's office. He had done it.

"Who's the best? You're the best," Connor said aloud.

The praise boosted him. He rolled to his feet, full of energy, and practically skipped through the open doorway.

It was time to see what all the fuss was about!

It *wasn't* time, however, to see the mop bucket that lay ahead of him. At least, not before he stepped in it.

"Waaahh!"

Connor lost his balance. He stumbled into a shelf. One of its items, a sort of dusky orb, pitched forward. It rolled the length of the shelf, hit a ledge and bounced to the floor.

SMASH.

The orb crumpled. Smoke shuddered into the air, rising high above Connor's shocked face.

CLEANING SPIRIT, LVL ??
Type: Deity
Skills: ??
Duration: ??

A set of angry eyes fixed on Connor.

"Who," said a low, rumbling voice, "are *you*?"

14
QUEST TRIGGER

CONNOR STARED AT THE SMOKE. WAS IT A cursed soul? A rare Gas-type fiend? No. He rubbed his eyes and exhaled.

"Just a Cleaning Spirit," he said with relief.

"*Excuse me?*" The smoke quivered, showing eyes bright as emeralds. "My name is Sir William, the All-Knowing Wisp, and when my powers return, I shall punish your insolence!"

Connor stared. "Your name is Willy ... the Wisp?"

"*Sir William!* Nevermind. Who are you? DON'T TOUCH THAT!"

Connor backed away from a shimmering, molten gold bottle. It stood alone on a shelf between large racks of chemicals, mop heads and sponges.

"Where is that foolish man, Oldentone?" Sir William demanded.

Connor hesitated. "He's, uh — it's kind of a long story."

Connor told the Wisp what had happened, beginning with the exploding door and Mr. Oldentone's pursuit of the Level 5 Slime. Sir William didn't say a word. At least, not until Connor reached the part with the—

"TIME LOOP!" Sir William roared. "Who told you about a time loop? WHO TOLD YOU?" His emerald eyes did a somersault.

"No one," Connor insisted. "I *lived* it. It's like this weird bug."

Sir William gave him a long look.

"It is no bug. The loop you describe is one of VGL's deepest secrets. It is a last resort. An emergency option."

"*Emergency?*"

"In a moment of grave danger, the VGL world will reboot automatically. The memories of most users will reset to an earlier state. Only the Custodian will remember. This is to assist in the Cleansing process. Should a Cleansing repeatedly fail, the Custodian may indeed experience a limited time loop effect until the threat is resolved."

"Does that mean *you* brought us into the loop?" Connor asked.

"Not I," said Sir William. "The server selects its Custodian. What puzzles me is how it made such a glaring mistake. *Choosing you.*"

Connor felt the Wisp's eyes upon him.

Judging him.

"How do you know I wasn't picked for a reason?" Connor said defensively. "Because of, uh—" he searched for a word, "my *abilities*. And stuff."

Sir William laughed. "Your abilities? *You?*"

A text box appeared in the air.

LAMB, CONNOR — STUDENT, LVL 2
Role: None
Abilities: None
Modifiers: + Speed, - Strength
Rank: E (#856 of 1000)

Connor winced. He tried to look away, but the text box followed his eyes like a sunspot.

Student, Level 2. Rank E.

"Oldentone was the *sensible* choice," Sir William sniffed. "As Custodian, he should have been chosen. Perhaps when you and he crossed paths, the VGL server malfunctioned? But that is *highly* unlikely. The game code would need to be altered directly ..."

Altered directly?

Connor thought of Lisa and her cheat codes. His eyes stretched to moons.

"Uh, about that," he said awkwardly.

• • • ● • ● • • •

"A HACKER! IN THE VGL WORLD!"

Sir William was still shouting five minutes later.

"It's *outrageous!* Our world has been infiltrated, and the villain hides in plain sight, posing as one of our students!"

"She *is* a student," said Connor.

He almost regretted telling Sir William about Lisa's hacking ability. The only good thing was that, between outbursts, Sir William had finally pieced together what had happened.

It began with the Slime.

When Lisa removed the Spectral Ooze from their avatars, she had exploited a flaw in VGL's security. In the process, important lines of code were changed or even erased. The server became so confused, it mistook Connor and Lisa for Custodians. So when disaster struck, it ended up looping *them* by mistake.

However, it hadn't looped Glitch. Which seemed odd. But when had Glitch's avatar ever made sense? If anything, he probably confused the server even more.

That was Sir William's opinion, at least.

"Your friend Lisa has put the entire server at risk!" he growled. "She must be punished. *Severely.* Once my powers are fully restored …"

Connor sighed. He felt bad for Lisa. He really did. But just then, he had bigger concerns.

"How do we *stop* the loop?" he asked the Wisp. "I'm sick of living the same school day over and over. I have after-school plans, you know? Swords to swing. Monsters to hunt."

Sir William stared at him.

"You fail to understand the situation," he said gravely. "The loop is a signal. It means the VGL world is in grave danger. Before the loop closes, the danger *must be resolved!*"

"So how do we resolve it?" said Connor.

"*You* don't. You are far too weak!"

An orb floated into the air. It was larger than a cleaning token, but smaller than the dusky orb that Connor had smashed.

"You will present this orb to the Custodian," said Sir William. "It contains a piece of my staggering intellect. I will handle the rest. I sense Oldentone's health running low, but little else. A strange fog clouds our bond. I must attend him in person."

"Where do we find him?" Connor started to ask. But he broke off with a "Whoaaa!"

A text box lunged at his eyeballs!

QUEST TRIGGER!

Sir William requires assistance. An orb containing a wisp of his spirit essence must be carried across campus and delivered to Mr. Oldentone, the Custodian. Simple, right? So why do you have such a bad feeling?

WARNING! Fiends detected! Battle may occur any time.

Do you accept?
Y / N

Connor's mouth fell open.

A Quest Trigger? *On school grounds?*

"Well?" said Sir William. "What are you waiting for? Tap Y to accept, boy!"

"I did," Connor insisted. "Nothing changed, it's not—" his voice sputtered. "My Vid-Glove! It won't let me do the Quest! It's switched off!"

A timer floated over the text.

WARNING! This Quest will expire in:

15 seconds ...
14 seconds ...
13 seconds ...

"No!" Connor shouted. "No, no, no, no!"

15
CLEANSING

THERE WERE LOUD SQUEAKS. CONNOR shimmied down the invisible chute. His palms burned. He moved so fast, he was *falling*.

THUMP. He crashed to the floor.

"WARNING! Health reduced by thirty percent," said a voice.

Connor groaned. And then, as he rolled to his feet, something *crunched*. He looked down. The orb had shattered. There was a rush of smoke and a furious voice.

"CRUSHED! CRUMPLED!" Sir William's eyes sprang to life. "Useless boy, you should have placed my token in storage!"

"I-I couldn't store it," Connor stammered, "my Vid-Glove—"

"And why have you *still* not accepted my quest? Suu Almighty! To think VGL's fate is in the hands of A NOOB!"

Glitch and Lisa were dumbstruck.

"Who *is* that?" they whispered.

"No time!" said Connor. He thrust his Vid-Glove at Lisa. "Can you hack it? Can you make it turn on?"

"You seek aid from A HACKER?" Sir William roared.

Lisa's eyes slitted.

"Ignore him!" Connor begged. "Please, my Quest Trigger is about to expire!"

"You got a Quest Trigger? *In Main Hall?*"

Connor nodded furiously. Lisa got the message. Even as she scowled, her fingers danced in the air.

"Power on," Connor's Vid-Glove reported.

Connor had never mashed a Y button faster.

QUEST ACCEPTED!

"Yes!" Connor whooped.

Sir William floated above Glitch's avatar. He was sniffing the air like a dog on a scent.

That can't be good, Connor thought. He was about to intervene when Lisa stopped him.

"Ahem." She motioned to Sir William. "*Explain.*"

· · · ● ● · ● ● · ·

CONNOR'S EXPLANATION TOOK SEVERAL minutes. By the time he had finished, the last spiky pixel was zooming toward the Wisp's swirling mouth.

There was a slurping sound.

"Disgusting," said Glitch.

"But effective," Lisa pointed out. "He ate those glitches like candy. Even the game code looks back to normal. Is he really just a Cleaning Spirit?"

Sir William burped loudly.

"I am a Deity-type powerhouse," he bragged. "My existence is miles above a mere Cleaning Spirit, although such lesser beings and I do share a—" he paused to burp again, *"family resemblance."*

Connor looked in awe at the revitalized Main Hall. Was this what Sir William had meant by a *Cleansing*? The locker doors sparkled. The ceiling was smooth and undamaged. Even the Potions Machine had stopped trembling. Although on closer inspection, the view from the windows looked strange …

Gone were the bright hills and sloping paths of VGL's campus. A whirl of movement replaced them, as if time had been set on fast-forward.

Connor rubbed his eyes. The view slowly spun back to normal.

Weird, he thought.

Sir William zoomed in circles beside the lockers. He looked extremely pleased with himself. Turning to address the group, or perhaps to brag even more, he gave a sudden moan.

His smoke body shivered.

There were loud bleeps and staticky cracks.

"Sir William? Are you all right?" said Connor.

"F-Fine," choked the Wisp. "I can exist in this form for up to one hour. Now that you've summoned me, disregarding my *clear instructions*, I'm taking charge of your Quest. No more mess ups. Even at my reduced level, I ... I ..."

Sir William's next word was hiccup. His mouth gurgled. It began to swirl in reverse.

"Uh oh," said Connor.

"Probably something he ate," Lisa whispered.

Sir William was shaking all over.

"He's gonna blow!" shouted Glitch. He grabbed the other two and started pulling them toward the exit. Lisa hesitated. But one look told Connor all that he needed.

"Run!" he cried.

Connor, Glitch and Lisa shot up the hall. They hit the exit door at a sprint and kept running. Wind howled at their backs. A chorus of bleeps, hisses and cracks chased them up the hill overlooking Main Hall as a deafening boom split the air.

"Aaaahhhhh!" shouted everyone.

Waves from the blast launched them upward. Their avatars turned somersaults, twisting and whirling, before finally landing in a heap of bent limps. Connor was the first to crawl out. He looked backward and gasped.

"That can't be *Main Hall*," Glitch's voice said beside him.

It was a sight beyond imagining. Main Hall, one of the largest buildings on campus, had completely collapsed. What remained looked less a building than a lump of pixels and weird, glitchy spikes.

Sir William's Cleansing had backfired, *big time.*

Lisa jumped to avoid a cartwheeling pixel. "Ew," she said, "glitch vomit."

"Keep me out of this, will you?" Glitch muttered.

Connor, who had been staring at Main Hall since the blast, finally cringed and looked away. The view left him dizzy. It was like staring up at the sun. Either that or an angry porcupine.

Glitch turned to Lisa. "So, about hacking other peoples' Vid-Gloves," he began to ask.

"Sorry, even I can't fix you," Lisa replied.

"I knew it," Glitch sighed.

With a tap, Connor summoned his Quest Map. Sir William's orb might have cracked, but the Quest, at least, was still active. A shimmering square stretched before him, with an X to mark his destination.

The X was closer than he expected.

"The Armorer's Tent?" said Glitch, reading over his shoulder.

Connor shook his head. "Just past it, I think. The shortcut with the weird weather. Mr. Oldentone must be Cleansing it."

"Think it's related to the time loop?"

"Could be. But what's the connection?"

"*Guys*," Lisa hissed suddenly.

Connor pointed to the Quest Map. "Lisa, look, you should see this—"

"No, *you* should see this."

Lisa flicked a finger. Her own Vid-Screen shot sideways, knocking the Quest Map away.

"Hey!" said Connor, while a grinning Glitch shouted, "Nice one!"

Lisa wasn't smiling, however. She jerked a thumb at the screen.

"Two fifty four," she said.

"Huh?"

"Is that, like, your PIN number?"

Connor and Glitch exchanged glances. Lisa strummed the air. Her Vid-Screen enlarged to show a ticking clock.

Two fifty four, it said, local time.

"W-What! How!?" Glitch spluttered.

"You know what this means?" said Lisa. "We don't have six hours. We have *six minutes* until the day loops again."

Connor uttered a moan.

He started to run.

16
COLD FRONT

CONNOR, GLITCH AND LISA WERE STILL arguing as they approached the Armorer's Tent.

"There isn't *time* for the Quest," Lisa insisted. "We should split up and try to see as much as we can before the day loops again. We'll compare notes in the morning."

"Ahem," said Glitch.

"Except for Glitch," Lisa added. "He's useless."

Glitch made a face. "I still don't get where the time went," he said. "Over five hours passed. How did we miss that?"

Connor sighed. He explained what he'd seen in the window.

"You think time outside of Main Hall *sped up*?"

"Ugh. Sir William is the worst!"

Everyone agreed about that, at least, as the Armorer's Tent rose into view. A mound of snow clogged the entrance flap. Glitch wiped the frost creeping over his goggles, amazed. Even Lisa looked shocked.

Connor filled them in on the changing weather patterns.

"I've always wondered about this shortcut," said Lisa. "It crosses over a chasm, right? But what's down below? It could be affecting the climate."

"Great sledding weather, though." Glitch peered around. "Hey, is that my shield?"

A chunk of furry metal sat atop the armorer's junk heap. It looked particularly foul, like a rotted mushroom.

"I ruined it, didn't I?" Glitch said gloomily.

"Not so loud," Connor warned. "The armorer might hear us. Speaking of which, let me duck behind you real quick ..."

But Connor's fears were misplaced. The tent, it seemed, was deserted. They found no hint of the armorer, nor anyone else, as they entered.

Icicles clung to the sales racks and drooped from the ceiling, while the ground was so cold, they heard warning chimes.

ALERT! FROZEN GROUND!
Health will decrease without proper equipment.

Lisa grabbed a pair of Level 5 boots off a rack. She held the boots out to Connor. "Here."

Connor hesitated.

"It's not *stealing*," said Lisa. "Watch."

She twirled a finger. The boots blurred. There were short *pops* as three additional pairs sprang to life, each identical to the first. Lisa returned the original boots with a smirk.

"An item dupe? You can *do* that?" said Glitch.

Lisa was grinning now. "They won't last forever," she admitted. "The game polices for duplicate items. But we should have a few minutes, at least, before the hash collides."

"What's a hash?" said Connor and Glitch.

Lisa made a nevermind gesture. She checked the clock.

"Two minutes left," she announced. "Let's hit the shortcut. You said Mr. Oldentone is definitely out there, Connor?"

"Should be." Connor summoned his Quest Map. The tiny X for Mr. Oldentone was indeed close. *Beyond* close, in fact. According to the map, the Custodian's current location was ...

"Inside the tent?"

Connor cast around with wide eyes. Lisa did the same with her Vid-Screen, while Glitch started probing the items at random. He brushed the snow off what looked like a full suit of armor.

"Brrrrr!" it wheezed, sending Glitch skidding backward.

The suit of armor began to shake. Chunks of snow fell to the floor, exposing a layer of hardened blue slime, which fell, too.

"Mr. Oldentone?" said everyone.

The Custodian looked awful. Blue liquid oozed down his skin, and his stiff eyebrows resembled the bristles on his broom weapon. It was easy to tell, because he was *holding* the broom. Its silver shaft looked majestic, even with half its bristles in knots.

Wow, Connor thought. He reached for the broom. He just wanted to feel it!

WARNING! Cannot interact with item "Oldentone's Broom."

Reason: Role Mismatch

"I'm not allowed?" Connor groaned.

"*Quiet*," Lisa shushed him. "What did you see, sir? Was it bad?" she asked Mr. Oldentone.

"Too — strong," he wheezed. "Even at full power I — failed to defeat it."

He strummed his lips, and the hitch in his voice disappeared.

"The enemy is a Fanged Slime. Or rather, it *was* one, before it evolved. Through unknown means, a party of Slimes bypassed VGL security this morning. I thought I had rounded them up. But no. One of the Slimes reached the Mainframe and found a method of leeching life from it. Slimes are mindless fiends, normally. So you can imagine my shock when this Slime used its fangs like a vampire. *Who taught it to do that?*"

Mr. Oldentone sighed.

"Flush with power, the Slime's level grew rapidly. Within minutes I was no longer its match. My avatar was smothered in ooze and left to rot. *Me*. The Custodian!"

"How do we stop it?" asked Lisa.

"Not to worry," said Mr. Oldentone. "I may be old, but I always win in the end. Let's just say the server has a plan for me." He waggled his eyebrows.

"Uh, it might not," Connor muttered.

Mr. Oldentone wasn't listening. He was already planning his loop.

"Perhaps if I act sooner — it means losing a relic, but I *could* take the Gold Disinfectant from my office and apply it to—"

ZZZZ!

Mr. Oldentone's voice stopped in mid-sentence. His avatar blinked and dissolved. A text box replaced his bald head.

Avatar "OLDENTONE, JONAS" Has Expired!
Reason: Corrosive Slime (Chip Damage)
Timeout: 600s
Respawn: Detention

The tent trembled. Icicles snapped from the ceiling as heavy sounds shook the floor.

"The Fanged Slime," Lisa whispered.

"Or whatever it evolved into," Glitch muttered.

Everyone stared at the shortcut. Connor was sure he heard squishing from the icy, dark exit flap. Glitch shut his eyes, then immediately wailed and reopened them.

"I can't take the suspense. I have to *know!*" he cried, rushing across the ice in his Level 5 boots.

Connor received a ping from his Vid-Glove.

QUEST LOG UPDATED!

Doh! You failed to deliver Sir William's orb to Mr. Oldentone, the Custodian. Instead you discovered a Fanged Slime has been leeching life from the VGL Mainframe. Not good! Hope is not lost, however. A chat with Mr. Oldentone offers a clue. If only you had a little more time. Wink, wink.

Find item "Gold Disinfectant" and deliver it to the Custodian. The sooner, the better. This Fanged Slime seems to level up quickly. You will have to move fast ...

"AAAAAHHHH!" cried a voice.

Connor looked up to find Glitch rushing out of the shortcut, chased by a horde of tiny Slime fiends.

More Slimes?

Could the Fanged Slime — *reproduce?*

It was Connor's last thought. A second later, the Slimes were upon him. He triggered his Wolf Buster Sword, then felt a chill as he remembered he'd lost it.

It didn't matter.

There were too many.

Connor swung his fists. He kicked crazily. But he soon felt the sting of slime toxins — the nibble of tiny, sharp fangs —

His vision went white.

The next thing he heard was a SCRITCH.

17

TIME LOOP 2.0

FIVE MINUTES LATER, CONNOR WAS zooming through space. His body twisted and turned. Then came a rushing sound.

"Waaaah!" Connor yelled.

He swiveled his hips. Relying on past experience, he stuck a two-footed landing even *gymnasts* would gawk at.

BOOOM!

Lisa's avatar crashed beside him, as clumsy as ever. Connor didn't wait for the smoke to clear this time. He stomped over.

"I can't *believe* what you said," Connor snapped. "Ms. Vickers was fuming! She thinks I *agreed* with you!"

Lisa groaned and sat up, wafting smoke from her eyes. "We were in a hurry," she said. "Why be nice when a few words get us thrown out of class right away?"

"A *few words*?" said Connor. "Lisa, you called our teacher a—"

"I know what I said," Lisa cut him off with a wave, "and I'm just warming up. Next loop, I'll get us zapped even faster. What can I say? I'm a power gamer at heart." Lisa beamed at him.

"On that note, we should probably get moving. I guess we'll follow your Quest, since it updated. So you need to fetch an item from Mr. Oldentone's office?"

"The Gold Disinfectant, yeah."

Lisa nodded. "Then we repeat everything. All our actions. It's the only way to be certain you'll get through the door. Oh, and Connor? Don't leave me hanging."

With a mad laugh, Lisa threw Mr. Oldentone's door open, touched a balloon-looking pixel and froze.

Connor's jaw hung open. Yes, he knew the plan was to save time where possible, in case they needed it later. But Lisa's quick moves left him dizzy. Events were unfolding too fast!

Connor inhaled a breath. He watched as Lisa floated in the open doorway, awaiting her rescue. Talk about speed-running. Lisa was on a whole different level.

He needed to get his head in the game.

They had work to do.

· · · ● · ● · · ·

KA-CHING! THE LEVEL 2 Fanged Slime flopped in half. Connor dropped the heavy sword and avoided a fall this time. *Barely.* The force of his swing sent him stumbling forward. He drove his feet through the goopy remains.

A message floated into the air.

ENEMY DEFEATED!
FANGED SLIME, LVL 2
+ 22 XP, + 5 Flux
Drops: None

Connor's heart pounded.

He'd almost forgotten the fiend in Main Hall!

A trail of mist rose from the floor. The fallen Wolf Buster Sword was dissolving. Connor sighed. He hated losing the sword. But he didn't dare skip the fight. Not after the disastrous events of their last loop.

What if *another* Fanged Slime reached the Mainframe? No. He could not let it happen!

After leaving Main Hall, Connor skipped the shortcut and took the Fiend Fountain path to Glitch's school building. He avoided Mr. Lively's classroom, heading straight for Glitch's locker.

He threw it open.

"*Empty?*" said Connor.

"Help! Help!" a voice rang out.

Connor yelped in surprise. But he was laughing once he found the *right* locker (his memory had been off by three doors) and swung it open, pulling his best friend into the hallway.

Glitch did not disappoint. As expected, he had no memory of the time loop, Sir William or anything.

Connor was about to explain, but he stopped.

"You'll find out soon enough," he told Glitch.

And he did.

· · · ● ● · ● · · · ·

"WHOOOOAAAAA!"

Glitch was screaming as the time field ejected him. Connor stuck a leg out to stop him tumbling down the hallway.

"It's over! It finally ended! I'm out!"

Glitch crawled to his knees, launching into a rant about lockers and clipping through walls. But before it ended—

BANG!

The time field collapsed. Pixels bounced up the halls, tangling and twisting as the hallway warped beyond all recognition.

Glitch's eyes boggled. He sprang to his feet.

"WHAT IS GOING ON?" he cried.

"Uh," said Connor.

He was grateful when Lisa stepped in to explain the finer details of looping to Glitch. Apparently Pfluter was involved somehow.

Shocking.

"Power on," Connor's Vid-Glove said randomly. Connor jumped in alarm.

"You're welcome," laughed Lisa. "You forgot Ms. Vickers shuts them off every loop, didn't you?"

Connor's face reddened. He *had* forgotten.

"Don't you have a Quest to do?" asked Lisa.

She pointed to Mr. Oldentone's doorway. It was floating again.

"Oh. Right!" Connor summoned his Quest Log. *Whew*, he thought. *Still active.*

Unlike stored items, which reset every loop, Connor's Quest Log had stayed the same. He supposed it made sense. Otherwise couldn't they grab the Gold Disinfectant, wait a while, then start a fresh loop with the item already in storage?

Talk about next level tactics.

You couldn't save more time than that!

Connor was so pleased with this concept (even though it wouldn't work) that he bragged about it to Glitch and Lisa as he shimmied up the walls.

"Genius!" said Glitch.

"It's not genius," Lisa said impatiently, "because it *doesn't work.*"

Connor sighed. "You'll never understand me."

About a minute later, he reached the top and looked down. He saw Glitch probing a row of spiked pixels. Lisa stood behind him, shouting,

"Just a few more! No, *that* one. See if you can *glitch* a way out!"

She suddenly paused and looked up.

"Remember the plan!" she yelled to Connor. "Get in. Get out. And most importantly—"

"Don't summon Sir William," Connor finished.

They'd been over this before. Deity or not, Sir William was too big a risk. He was unpredictable. What if he tried to Cleanse the hallway again? His last attempt had cost them six hours! Not to mention it had toppled Main Hall ...

Connor stepped gingerly into Mr. Oldentone's office. He dodged the mop bucket and kept from bumping the shelves.

His heart pounded.

There it was. Unmissable. On a shelf all its own.

The Gold Disinfectant.

Connor drew in a breath. It was magnificent. Was this a bottle of cleaning solution or the loot from some high-level dungeon?

The bottle was tall and thin, like a flute. Molten gold sloshed within, crisp as moonlight, while a lemon scent rose from the stopper.

Connor inched closer. His stomach swirled. He felt anxious just *breathing*.

"It's only a bottle," he reminded himself. "Stop time-wasting."

He took a last breath and reached for it.

WHOOSH. An unseen force sent him staggering back!

> **WARNING! Cannot interact with item "Gold Disinfectant."**
>
> **Reason: Role Mismatch.**
> *ALERT! The Guardian has been notified.*

"What! WHAT!"

Connor spun around so quickly, it was a miracle he didn't bump any shelves. Not that he needed to.

Smoke was rising around him.

A pair of emerald eyes opened.

18
THE GUARDIAN

"MY NAME IS SIR WILLIAM, THE ALL-Knowing Wisp. As Guardian of all things Custodial, I will ask you one time, boy: *what are you doing here?*"

"Uh," said Connor.

His mind raced. *Sir William doesn't recognize me. His memory must have been wiped by the loop. But then — what do I do?*

What *could* he do?

"Fiend got your tongue? Be thankful my orb is intact. If you had smashed it, I would have used my full power to punish you. You would be dust for the Custodian's broom!"

"You don't *have* your full power," Connor said automatically.

He cupped his mouth. He knew at once that he'd made a mistake.

Sir William went very still.

"N-Nonsense!" he stammered. "Who told you that? WHO TOLD YOU?"

Connor's heart pounded. He'd said the one thing he couldn't explain! Not if he wanted to keep the time loop a secret.

Think, Connor, think! Who else knew about Sir William? What name would make Sir William believe him?

Connor's mind shook. "M-Mr. Oldentone!" he blurted out. "Mr. Oldentone told me all about you. He said you were, uh, very wise. And that soon you would regain your full powers. And also that — oh, right! He asked me to bring this item to him, sir, if I could."

Connor pointed to the Gold Disinfectant.

"Did he now?" Sir William mulled it over. "*If you could* … Are you quite sure? He used those precise words?"

No, Connor thought. *I just made that up.*

He didn't tell the Wisp that.

Instead he narrowed his eyes. Something in Sir William's tone made him pause. Apparently the words he'd used were important. They *meant* something.

Connor made up his mind. "Yes," he replied. "That's what he said. Mr. Oldentone."

It was almost true. Mostly true. Connor had an active Quest, after all ...

"How intriguing." Sir William's eyes gleamed. "The old man would have known that *you,* a measly Level 2 student, could not lay a hand on a relic. As for removing the stopper and actually *using* it — never! You are not trained in Custodial Arts."

"Can't you just, uh, give it to me?" Connor said hopefully.

"Of course not. The Gold Disinfectant can only be taken, not given. Which begs the question: why ask this impossible task of you? What was Oldentone thinking?"

Sir William gave Connor a searching look. Connor's lip trembled. He had the impression his fate was being decided.

The Wisp made a tutting noise.

"Very well. I will play along, just this once."

ZZZZ!

Space tore, and a portal sprang to life in mid-air. A mix of shadow and light danced within, emitting a low hum that sent chills through Connor's avatar.

"What is it?" he asked.

"A test," said the Wisp. "With luck, perhaps more. Though do not get your hopes up. The mysteries of the Custodial Arts are beyond your current abilities. The most you can achieve is a minor proficiency: small success of the first level. Even that may be asking too much."

"I don't understand," said Connor.

Sir William sighed. "You seek the Gold Disinfectant, but you lack the qualifications to claim it. Specifically, the 'Custodian' role. I do not know why Oldentone chose you to help him. Perhaps he did not. Perhaps this is one big mistake. We shall see."

The Wisp glanced at the portal.

"Inside is the Custodial World, Level 1. It is a training world for future Custodians. You must clear five scenarios. For a gifted apprentice, the estimated time-to-complete is sixty hours. For a *prodigy* such as yourself, however—" Sir William gave a snort, "perhaps you can do it in thirty."

Connor's stare was as blank as one of his quiz sheets. "THIRTY HOURS?" he cried.

"*If* you're lucky. *If* your talent is one-in-a-million. For a student lacking in talent, even a hundred hours would not be enough."

Connor's heart raced. *This can't be happening,* he thought.

Sir William saw his terror and laughed.

"Foolish boy. Did you imagine you could complete this task in one day? Is that how you view the Custodial Arts? As just a small thing? A stepping stone? No. The Custodial Arts are the mop and broom that keep the VGL world running smoothly, and fiend-free!

"Now then, as this work will exhaust you, I suggest we limit our sessions to one hour each—" Sir William's voice stopped abruptly. "Boy, where are you running off to?"

"Uh, just a minute!" said Connor.

He made a dash to the exit. Shoving his head through the doorway, he stared down the cliff and yelled, "Guys? We have a serious problem!"

19
THIRTY HOURS

"BUT THIS IS PERFECT!" SAID LISA. "AS A matter of fact, I was going to suggest the same thing myself. We have the time. Why not use it?"

She pointed to an exit door with at least a dozen sharp spikes surrounding it. One of the spikes looked a bit flatter.

One.

"Glitch and I *are* making progress," Lisa insisted, "but it's slow going. Sort of trial and error."

"Mostly error," said Glitch.

"No, no, you just need more practice," said Lisa. "It's not easy to control Glitch's power," she told Connor, "but with time, we can *definitely* clear a path out of Main Hall. I know it."

Connor sighed. He was back in the hallway now. But when he'd shimmied down for a chat with Glitch and Lisa, he'd been counting on reactions like, "Thirty hours? Nah, dude," or "Forget it, we'll find a quicker solution."

At least some kind of sympathy.

Not *excitement*. Not Lisa all but jumping for joy.

"It's just, I'm learning *so much*," she gushed. "Glitch's Vid-Glove is like a miracle. I never knew. You should see the *chaos* he brings to the game code."

Lisa even had a plan sorted out.

"Okay, here's what I'm thinking. Glitch and I will continue working down here while you, Connor, do your Quest thing. Whatever it takes to advance it."

"But *thirty hours?*" said Connor. "That means multiple loops!"

"I *know*, it'll be just like a video game!" Lisa grinned. "Each loop, we'll use our knowledge to work smarter and faster. We'll repeat our actions up to the point you meet with Sir William. Then we'll blitz toward the finish.

"Once Glitch and I get out of Main Hall (and we *will* get out) we'll scout the area. I'll find out exactly where Mr. Oldentone is, what level the Fanged Slime is at, how it's feeding, even how fast it gains experience."

Lisa's avatar shook with delight.

"Oh, this is so much more fun than a field trip!"

"Yeah, fun," Connor grumbled.

He took his time climbing back to Sir William. His heart ached. He would've *loved* to stay and pop spikes with Glitch and his Vid-Glove.

But no. He had a date with Sir William.

FOR THIRTY HOURS.

True, he might earn a role by the end of it. Roles were hype — they gave huge benefits. But in his head, Connor had always imagined his role as something awesome, like Blood Mage or Dread Pirate Ninja.

Definitely not Custodian, which sounded no fun at all. It was almost like going back to Ms. Vickers's classroom.

Maybe worse than that.

And for *way* longer.

"Ah, the apprentice returns," said Sir William as Connor slumped his way into the office. "Are you ready to work? Will you claim your role? Seize your weapon?"

Connor, who had been slouching before, stood straight up.

"W-Weapon? I get a weapon? Me?"

Sir William blew a line of smoke at the portal. It swelled in response until it loomed over Connor like a crack in the universe.

"Enter and see," said the Wisp. "One of my fragments will meet you inside, and together we will study—"

Light and smoke fused together.

"THE SACRED BROOM ART!"

20
STUBBORN

AS CONNOR STEPPED THROUGH THE portal, he felt a tingling sensation. His heart pounded. Then—

FWOOSH. He shot forward!

CUSTODIAL WORLD, DAY ONE

BANG.

Connor landed hard on both feet. Thanks to his reflexes, he merely stumbled a bit, but stayed standing. He peered around.

And felt his hype melt away. Was this a joke?

"There's nothing but empty space!"

Connor's shoulders slumped. Had Sir William lied to him? Where were the fiends? The cool weapons?

Suddenly the air trembled. The empty space tore like cloth, reminding Connor of a video game when new content was loading. One by one, objects sprang up around him.

He saw leafy trees. Gravel paths. A wooden hut with a round porch and several large tables, fully loaded with plates, cups and food.

A text box loomed over them.

SCENARIO 1-1
["Camp Oshawaka: Lunch"]

There was just time to think, *Weird*. Then the words vanished, and Camp Oshawaka erupted.

An unseen force swept the scene like a hurricane.

BANG! BOOM! SPLAT!

Connor threw himself to the ground as a water jug fizzed past his ear. Plates spun like Frisbees while cups, like kernels of popcorn, jumped skyward, their contents raining down over everything.

Somehow the hut took the worst of it. Wind whipped in loops, flinging napkins at windows. Ketchup gummed to the reedy roof thatches while one of the tables, which had flipped upside down, wedged itself into the entrance.

A last gust of wind brought a message.

OBJECTIVE: CLEAR THE PORCH!
Mrs. Delaphon's first-grade class had a picnic, and they've left quite a mess behind. Forget fiends for a moment. How can you call yourself a Custodian if you can't handle a group of rowdy seven-year-olds? (Time limit: 600s)

Begin Tutorial Mode?
Y / N

(Note: clock will not stop)

Connor stared in amazement. A large clock had appeared with the message.

600 ...
599 ...
598 ...

He felt a rush of adrenaline.

"No time, no time!"

He tapped the N button. "Good luck, apprentice!" a voice echoed, as the entire porch (including the hut) flashed a blinding bee-yellow.

This must be the zone I'm meant to clear, Connor thought. But *how* could he clear it?

There was a rushing sound. As if reading his thoughts, the game sent a large item fizzing his way. Connor caught it smoothly, felt the stiff bristles and groaned.

He almost couldn't believe it.

BEGINNER'S BROOM, LVL 1
Type: Cleaning Weapon
Rarity: D
Durability: D

Additional Information: What are three things worse than a Level 1 Slime? Dust, dirt and grime! Attack the worst messes so your classmates don't have to. No role required. Just effort!

"A *cleaning* weapon? For *beginners*?"

It was beyond miserable. The Beginner's Broom was a dreary dust-brown, nothing like the majestic pole Mr. Oldentone carried. Judging by the bent bristles, it was not even new.

How could a *used* broom be a weapon? How could it compare to an axe or a sword? Or even a crossbow?

Connor stalked around, sweeping the porch with rough strokes. His heart wasn't in it. He was almost glad when his clock ran out.

TIME IS UP!
SCENARIO 1-1 FAILED!

Camp Oshawaka turned a misty gray color. So did Connor's avatar. For several seconds he wandered the scene like a lonely ghost.

Then he screamed.

"Aaaah!"

Sir William beamed to life, tutting loudly.

"A pathetic attempt. Defeated on the opening mission. And you call yourself a prodigy?"

"I never said that. *You* did," Connor growled. "You also said I'd get a weapon. But it was just an old broom!"

"When used *correctly*," said Sir William, "even a Beginner's Broom can work wonders. But how would *you* know? You skipped the Tutorial."

"I had to," said Connor. "The clock—"

"Oh, *the clock*." Sir William spat smoke at Connor's eyes. "The Sacred Broom Art is wasted on brats like you, truly. Tell me, why should I teach you?"

Connor hesitated.

"I *could* give you pointers, you know," said the Wisp. "But in return what would I get? How about your undying loyalty? Yes! Bow down to me. *Beg* for my brilliant advice!"

"No way!" Connor's eyes slitted. He wasn't bowing to anyone, he decided, least of all Sir William.

A text box hovered between them.

TRY AGAIN?
Y / N

Still eyeing Sir William, Connor smashed the Y button. He smirked as the Wisp vanished (the game world had booted him) and SCENARIO 1-1 reappeared, full of color and light.

And soon enough—
BANG! BOOM! SPLAT!
Flying food.

· · · ● ● · ● ● · · ·

TIME IS UP!
SCENARIO 1-1 FAILED!

"Argh!"

TIME IS UP!
SCENARIO 1-1 FAILED!

"NO!"

TIME IS UP!
SCENARIO 1-1 FAILED!

"WHY IS THIS HAPPENING!"

Connor hurled the Beginner's Broom like a spear. It sailed across the porch, which *still* looked a mess, even as the world turned to gray.

A text box loomed like a curse.

TRY AGAIN?
Y / N

"My offer is still on the table," said Sir William, who reappeared with a pop. "*Or* you could come to your senses and complete the Tutoria—"

THUMP. Connor slammed the Y button and the Wisp disappeared.

"Twenty-sixth time is the charm," he muttered under his breath.

It wasn't.

Connor had always been stubborn. Today, though, he'd pushed his stubbornness over the edge. He was *raging*. His brain had shrunk to the size of a cat hair.

Determined to clear **SCENARIO** 1-1 on his own, Connor ignored *all* of Sir William's advice. Especially Tutorial Mode. Doing *that* meant admitting defeat.

Nuh-uh. Not going to happen.

Fatigue was setting in. Although avatars in the VGL world were different from human bodies, they used realistic muscle responses. Connor's arms drooped. It was his thirtieth attempt to clear Camp Oshawaka (at least) and so far, his best strategy was also his most exhausting.

Sweat streamed down his face.

Ignoring the Beginner's Broom, which bobbed uselessly, Connor rushed around, dragging entire tables off the porch and into the woods. He hurled cups over treetops, delivered swift kicks to the plates, then swabbed the porch using only his heel and a napkin.

His chest heaved and his muscles were screaming. He'd never worked so hard in his life. Not even snow-shoveling! Nevertheless, two tables and several plates remained inside the yellow zone as time expired.

He had lost.

Connor's whole body slumped. He stared at his feet until something bumped the back of his neck. Expecting Sir William, he whirled around.

"Oww!"

A text box bounced off his forehead.

BONUS UNLOCKED!
Congratulations! You pushed hard and broke through your limits.

Perseverance Award: Stamina +1

Note: Modifier bonus; includes Stamina refill

"Holy bats!" Connor's eyes widened. He felt a surge of energy, even as Sir William materialized in front of him.

"What are you so glad about?" barked the Wisp. "With your speed, you could barely clean a land snail convention!"

Connor flexed his fingers, feeling the same rush of energy.

"Give me time," he murmured.

Grinning now, he tapped Y to restart.

21
TUTORIAL MODE

SIR WILLIAM ZOOMED AROUND the empty King's Castle. Though misty and gray, the carpets looked tidy. The royal throne even gleamed. The marble floor, however, was a sprawling, post-battle mess.

A message floated over the sword scars.

TIME IS UP!
SCENARIO 1-2 FAILED!

"Passable. For an apprentice, at least," said Sir William. "If I didn't know better, I'd say you'd done this before, boy."

Connor smirked.

He *had* done it before. Many times. Sir William just didn't remember.

It was Connor's first run of a new loop. With his Stamina bonus, he'd finally cleared Camp Oshawaka and reached SCENARIO 1-2, King's Castle.

"Don't smile yet," warned the Wisp. "You may have cleared SCENARIO 1-1, but your technique was atrocious. You have a toddler's grasp of the Sacred Broom Art. Without improvement, your road to Custodian stops here, at King's Castle."

We'll see, thought Connor.

Now that he'd unlocked King's Castle, he could think of a million improvements. He couldn't wait to try his run again.

"So long, Camp Oshawaka," Connor laughed.

He tapped the button to replay King's Castle.

The world blurred and distorted. But while color returned, the royal throne didn't. Instead there were leafy trees. Gravel paths. A familiar-looking hut with a—

"NO!" Connor yelled.

He stared in horror at the text box.

SCENARIO 1-1
["Camp Oshawaka: Lunch"]

"I have to start over? No way!"

Connor grabbed the Beginner's Broom that appeared and flung it into the hut. He crossed his arms and stood, glaring, as time ticked away.

If he couldn't permanently advance to King's Castle, what was the point? Was the Custodial World a torture dimension?

It wasn't *fun* rushing around like he did.

It was *work*.

Soon the world turned to gray.

TIME IS UP!
SCENARIO 1-1 FAILED!

Sir William floated up to him.

"You need to learn, boy. Custodians are not born. They are *made*, through deliberate practice."

Connor scowled. "I'm working as hard as I—"

FWOOSH.

The Beginner's Broom came flying out of the hut. It bopped Connor's nose in mid-speech.

Connor slapped it away.

"Only a fool ignores a weapon," said the Wisp.

"It's a *broom*," said Connor.

"It is many things," said Sir William. His smoke quivered, and the Beginner's Broom swelled with light. Its bristles made loud crackling sounds—

POP. They became the loose string of a mop. POP. The head of a vacuum. POP. A leaf blower. A stone shovel. A high-powered squirt gun.

"*What!* No one told me it did that!" said Connor.

Sir William wore a smug smile.

"Come to Tutorial Mode. Forget the clock. Failing a few runs is unimportant. Before you run, you must first learn to walk."

Custodial World, Day Three

CONNOR BLITZED THROUGH HIS movements.

"Mop on!" said the Tutorial.

Connor swung the Beginner's Broom in the swift downward arc he'd been taught. POP. The wooden pole flopped with yarn.

"Mop off!" said the Tutorial.

Connor swung the pole in reverse. POP. The silver bristles returned.

Connor smiled. By now he knew the movements by heart. He continued flawlessly through the transitions to Vacuum, Leaf Blower and more.

It was amazing how the Beginner's Broom shifted. Depending on the mode, a clean swing could lift stains, summon wind, or even deal damage directly. Even better, the Beginner's Broom drew its power from the Speed stat, not Strength, which suited Connor's avatar perfectly.

After a full loop spent drilling the basics, Connor's focus today was transitions. Certain shifts still eluded him, like the direct shift from Vacuum to Squirt Gun.

Strictly speaking, the Tutorial didn't teach this. Its lessons stuck to the basics: Broom to Mop, Mop to Vacuum and so on. With practice, however, Connor had found ways to switch from any one mode to another.

Now he wanted to push his technique to the limit.

Speed was key!

TUTORIAL MODE FAILED!
Are you even trying? Your moves went from hero to zero!

TRY AGAIN?
     Y / N

As the level turned gray, Connor laughed. So he'd flunked the Tutorial's "final exam" again. Big deal. The exam was long and annoying. He used the extra time for more practice.

Sir William was unimpressed. "I admit you have talent," he said grudgingly, "but your patience is lacking. You must learn to *follow instructions.*"

Then, several runs later:

"Boy, are your ears muted? Shall I brighten your eyes? What kind of FOOL flunks Tutorial Mode SEVEN TIMES?"

Seven? Try forty-seven, thought Connor.

He hit Y to restart.

After that, the Wisp stopped appearing. Connor didn't mind. He enjoyed the relative calm of Tutorial Mode. Not to mention his Sacred Broom Art was improving dramatically.

FWOOSH. He swung the Beginner's Broom, feeling a thick swirl of energy. His broom was a blur of motion. A wheel without end.

At some point, Sir William returned. He had come to gloat, it seemed. But as he tracked Connor's movements, his emerald eyes grew to moons.

"*Swift as lightning ... falls like rain ... leopard's leap ...*"

Sir William stared in amazement. He reveled in Connor's swift moves. Then, after a particularly tough sequence—

"*Good broom!*" cried the Wisp.

Hot with excitement, he rushed the course at the end of the session.

"Such speed! Such finesse! Did Oldentone teach you that? You are full of secrets, boy. I think I'm starting to like you!"

Sparks leapt from his eyes.

"Let's have a run at the course! What do you say? With your skill, you could reach SCENARIO 1-4, at least!"

Connor laughed at the Wisp's change of heart.

"No thanks," he replied. "With more practice, I can improve even more."

He felt sure.

THE TIME HAD COME, Connor decided. And it would come without warning — to Sir William, at least. The Wisp was a blithering mess, a shell of smoke, as Connor raised his broom in delight.

SCENARIO 1-5 CLEAR!

He had won! He'd cleared all five stages of the training world, even the ones he hadn't seen yet. He didn't fail once!

Connor gave a whoop of laughter. He swung his broom out, sending a gust of wind at the incoming text box, which swirled like a kite.

TRAINING WORLD COMPLETE!
Role "Custodian" Awarded (Rank E)
NEW! Can now interact with "Custodian" items
NEW! Will now receive @Custodian pings

RARE REWARD!
Ability unlocked: *Custodian's Call, Lvl 1*
Summon a cleaning token when you need one (cooldown: 3600s)

STATS:
Runs required: 1
Total time elapsed: 26 minutes, 6 seconds
[COURSE RECORD!]

Back in Mr. Oldentone's office, Connor found Sir William in shambles. The Wisp drifted from shelf to shelf, mumbling, *"Impossible ..."* and *"How could anyone ..."* and, in a quavering voice, *"What a monster ..."*

He saw Connor and jolted.

"Y-You're back. Y-You succeeded. Not — bad."

Connor grinned. He summoned his Stat Sheet.

LAMB, CONNOR — STUDENT, LVL 2
Role: Custodian (Rank E)
Abilities: *Custodian's Call, Lvl 1*
Modifiers: + Speed, + Stamina, - Strength
Rank: E (#856 of 1000)

Connor's heart swelled with triumph. His first role! His first ability, too! True, it bugged him a little that his rank hadn't changed. But farming loot and XP would be easy now, thanks to his fancy new—

Wait.

Connor scanned his inventory. The Beginner's Broom was not there. It had disappeared with the training world!

Connor's eyes narrowed. "I'm a Custodian now," he said aloud, "so where's my broom?"

"Your broom? YOUR OWN BROOM?"

Sir William zoomed up to Connor. The Wisp had regained his composure, and with it, his charming personality.

"Just because you perfectly passed the Custodial World, Level 1—" he began to lecture.

"I passed perfectly?" said Connor.

"Listen, brat!" Sir William swelled angrily. "You think passing the training world is an accomplishment? You earned your role today. Very well! But you are not fit to own a broom yet. Far from it!"

Connor gaped. The news hit him like a hand grenade.

"You mean I trained *four loops* for nothing?"

Sir William went very still.

"Loops? LOOPS, DID YOU SAY, BOY?"

His emerald eyes flashed. He seemed to make a few connections instantly, because a moment later, his smoke formed a grasping claw.

"Uh oh," said Connor.

He ducked the claw, grabbed the Gold Disinfectant and ran for the exit.

"Boy, get back here!"

Sir William hissed and gave chase.

22

THE LAST LOOP

FOUR SECONDS AND ONE FRANTIC, death-defying swan dive later, Connor hit the floor with a thump.

"WARNING! Health reduced by thirty percent," said a voice.

Connor glanced around the hallway island. Where were Lisa and Glitch? Where was *anything*? He dived left as a claw snatched the air. Sir William was hot on his heels!

"*Seize him!*" cried the Wisp.

"Seize who? Who *is* that?"

A pair of swim goggles burst through the floor.

Connor's heels skidded. "*Glitch?*"

His best friend grinned from inside a huge hole.

"We built a tunnel," Glitch said excitedly. "It was Lisa's idea. Way faster than surface work. Leads all the way to the exit door!"

Glitch pointed down the tunnel.

Connor was at a loss for words. Glitch and Lisa had finished their escape route? *Already?*

"Ow!" Connor yelped as the claw struck his neck. It was a glancing blow, but it knocked him sideways and into the tunnel.

Incredibly, he stuck a two-footed landing.

On top of Glitch.

"Ow. Ow," moaned Glitch. Connor hopped aside. He hauled Glitch to his feet by his bookbag straps.

"Not so rough! This bookbag has special cargo," said Glitch.

There was a rushing sound from above.

"Go, go!" Connor yelled. Glitch didn't argue. The boys fled down the tunnel.

Even as they ran, Connor had to admit, the tunnel was cool. The walls were high and wide: an odd mix of chipped, charred and punctured. The job wasn't pretty. But it worked wonderfully.

A short jog led Connor and Glitch through a hole in front of Main Hall's side exit.

A Vid-Screen bounced through the door as it opened. Glitch snapped his fingers and Lisa looked up. She saw Connor and grinned.

"You're back! Perfect timing! Did you get the — WHOOAH!"

Like a stone trap, a wall of darkness descended. The exit door disappeared as Connor, Glitch and Lisa found themselves trapped in a ring of black smoke.

A pair of emerald eyes flared within. The Wisp waved a smoldering claw.

"What is this *fiendish plot*?" Sir William demanded. "Damaging school property — defacing VGL game code — and you, boy! You speak of *time manipulation*? You will explain yourselves, or I will see you incinerated. Your avatars will be burned worse than a bad breakfast!"

Connor made a face. *Uh, that's weird.*

He glanced at Glitch and Lisa. Glitch, in particular, looked strange. As a non-looper, he shouldn't have remembered the Wisp. But Lisa had clearly told him *some* things, because he blurted out:

"Oh, you're Sir William! I heard about you. You're that Cleaning Spirit. The rude one with faulty powers."

Glitch touched the smoldering claw with his Vid-Glove. It immediately hissed and dissolved.

"WHAT SORCERY IS THIS!" roared Sir William. "WHO HAS BEEN — TELLING YOU — SECRETS?"

The ring of smoke tightened around them. Connor felt a burning sensation. He started to choke.

His thoughts raced. Was Sir William bluffing? Could he really — *destroy* them?

He decided he wasn't in the mood to find out. He glanced at Lisa, who gave a curt nod.

"Might as well — tell him," she gasped.

· · · ● ● ● ● · · ·

SIR WILLIAM WAS NOT amused. He listened to Connor's story with such thinly veiled rage that Connor even paused once to ask if he was feeling all right.

"*Go on,*" the Wisp snarled.

Connor's voice trembled as he finished his story. He glanced at Sir William. His smoke had sprouted thin spikes, so he rather resembled a hedgehog.

"We used the resets responsibly," Lisa insisted. "While Connor trained, I scouted the Mainframe. I met with Mr. Oldentone. I saw the Fanged Slime. I learned lots of important things in our loops."

"So did I," Glitch piped up. "Lisa's been filling me in. I think it's amazing. I know it's school still. But like — actually *fun*."

That did it.

"Fun. FUN? Do you think the Emergency Reset, VGL's last resort before code destruction, is a circus for your amusement? Are you ENJOYING yourselves?"

A Vid-Screen appeared with a pop. It formed an arc around Sir William, whose emerald eyes scanned the strange graphs and cryptic reports that beamed across it.

"System Control," he huffed. "Normally even I wouldn't bother to check this. Our security is top notch. But seeing as my bond to Oldentone has weakened, and after what you fools have just claimed, perhaps—"

His voice stopped abruptly. Sparks shot from his eyebrows.

"What is it?" said everyone.

"YOU! YOU'VE DOOMED US ALL!" cried the Wisp.

"He must be misreading. That can't be *English*," said Connor, eyeing the Vid-Screen.

Glitch stared through his swim goggles. He couldn't decipher the flashing text, either.

"*Amateurs*. Step aside."

Lisa pushed past them. Her eyes thinned. After a few seconds' reading, she gasped.

"What is it?"

Lisa pointed to what looked like an empty pie chart. She pinched to zoom and the words sprang to life.

EMERGENCY POWER CELL
Charge Remaining: 6%
WARNING! DOES NOT RECHARGE!

Requires min. 5% charge to reset (automatic)

"What! We're almost out of resets?" said Connor.

Lisa nodded grimly. "One left. I guess our loops weren't unlimited, after all."

"Of course not! How absurd!" Sir William's smoke seethed. "The Emergency Power Cell will take *years* to recharge, if it recharges at all. *You three*—" Sir William jerked a claw at them, "have wasted a precious resource. I hope you enjoy in-person schooling. Because when the VGL Mainframe *blows up*, that's your next destination!"

"No!" Connor cried. "I won't go back! They can't make me!"

Lisa and Glitch looked aghast.

23
SCOUTING REPORT

SIR WILLIAM FLEW TO THE EXIT.

"I'm leaving. I need to find Oldentone. With our powers combined, perhaps we can turn the tide on this nightmare. *Perhaps.*"

Lisa watched him go with a sigh.

"It won't help," she muttered. "I've seen what we're up against."

With a wave, she summoned a Vid-Screen. An image of Glitch beamed to life. His Vid-Glove did a funny shake, and the pixel it touched blew apart.

"Oops, wrong clip," said Lisa.

"So *that's* how you're teaching him!" said Connor. "You have recordings from Glitch's past loops. No wonder he's learning so fast."

Glitch smiled slyly.

A second clip appeared. It showed a Fanged Slime with its mouth around a large, glowing crystal. The crystal's light flickered.

"The Slime is draining its power!" said Connor.

Lisa nodded. In her next clip, the Slime bounced along the crystal, slurping more and more light. Its huge body swelled with each bite until—

POP.

A dozen smaller Slimes burst from its belly! Though low-leveled, they swarmed the crystal with tiny, sharp fangs.

"*The Slime army,*" Connor whispered.

His skin prickled. He remembered those guys. They had invaded the Armorer's Tent. It was *bad.*

"Where did you film this?" said Glitch. "It can't be the shortcut still. It's too dark."

"No, it's the shortcut. *Underneath,*" Lisa replied. "You know how the shortcut is this sort of land bridge across a chasm? That really deep hole?"

"Duh," said Connor.

"And you know that one twisting path no one takes? There's a big sign on it, "FORBIDDEN PASSAGE," and it veers off into darkness? I used to think it dead-ended. But no. It leads down. *All the way down*."

A light bulb went off in Connor's head.

"The Mainframe is down there!"

"Exactly," said Lisa. "The Mainframe powers the VGL world. It's huge and it sits in that chasm. I haven't worked out the details. But it's obvious what we're meant to do. We have to keep the Slimes off the crystals."

"What about Mr. Oldentone? Shouldn't he be helping?" said Connor.

He didn't see the Custodian anywhere.

"Funny you say that." Lisa triggered a fourth clip. The man who appeared looked a lot like a Slime fiend. Blue liquid flowed down his bald head and coated his clothes, which had hardened to form a spiky blue crust.

"Yep, he's frozen," said Lisa.

There was a sudden BOING. Mr. Oldentone's avatar shot skyward. His blue body shrank as it soared, fading into the clouds with a twinkle.

The Slime who bopped him roared savagely.

"The same thing happens each loop." Lisa sighed as she banished the clip. "At first, Mr. Oldentone and the Fanged Slime are evenly matched. But as time passes, the Slimes multiply. They grow bigger and faster. By nine fifteen, it's all over. Mr. Oldentone gets dunked in slime toxins. His avatar freezes up. And then, well …"

"He gets yeeted to the moon!" said Glitch, a little too enthusiastically.

Connor snickered.

"*Boys.*" Lisa rolled her eyes. "The point is, we have to arrive before then. Nine fifteen. That's our deadline."

"Then shouldn't we get a move on?" said Glitch.

Lisa shook her head. "I told you, it's too late for that. We're past nine fifteen, which means the Fanged Slime is already massive." She sighed. "We'll just have to complete Connor's Quest in the next loop. That's our best shot at saving the

Mainframe. Connor needs to deliver that item thing—"

"The Gold Disinfectant," said Connor.

"But what is it?" said Glitch.

"A power-up for Mr. Oldentone's broom," Lisa replied. "You spray it across the bristles or something. I don't know. Mr. Oldentone was sort of busy when I asked him about it. But it sounds promising. *If* Connor can deliver it in time."

"With our help, he will," said Glitch. "Lisa is pretty good from long range," he told Connor. "You should see her Vid-Screen recordings. She's scary. And I've, uh, got a few tricks as well."

Glitch peered through his goggles at Lisa.

"You *are* going to help me re-learn them, right?"

Lisa smiled innocently. "Of course I will."

Glitch didn't seem reassured.

"Ten o'clock," Lisa announced, checking her Vid-Screen. "Not that it matters. We have the full loop to work out our battle plan, which is good since we're going to need it. A lot has changed, Connor. I'll fill you in. But first, let's see this 'Gold Disinfectant.' You've got it in inventory, right?"

"Uh, yeah." Connor raised his Vid-Glove. Before he summoned the item, however, a noise rang out.

"What is *that*?" said everyone.

The locker doors trembled. A chorus of bleeps, hisses and staticky cracks rose from outside Main Hall.

Connor saw a whirl of movement in the windows. His heart sank.

"Not again!" he moaned. "It's got to be Sir William. That dork, he's attempting another Cleansing. Look!"

Glitch and Lisa followed his gaze. Their avatars swayed dizzily, watching a scene that zoomed along in fast-forward.

"My brain hurts," Glitch said queasily.

There were loud cracks. Then a *smash* as a ceiling tile hit the floor next to Lisa, who gasped.

"You know what this means?" she squeaked. "Time is speeding up again. It'll be three o'clock before we know it!"

CRACK. A fresh chunk of ceiling collapsed.

Connor was shaking his head. "It won't matter what time it is if the building caves in. One way or another, this loop is ending right now!"

Lisa nodded shakily.

"Get r-ready," she told Connor. "The day is about to reset. When it does, we move as fast as we can. Get to Main Hall. Grab the Gold Disinfectant. Give it to Mr. Oldentone. We have one shot at this. If we fail, that's the end. No more loops."

"No more VGL," Connor mumbled.

It was a fate worse than death. Virtual death, surely. He could not let it happen!

A mighty boom shook the building. Connor remembered it as the last sound before Main Hall had collapsed in a previous loop. His eyes widened. Even Lisa shook nervously.

Only Glitch seemed relaxed. Normally the opposite of cool and collected, he calmly unzipped his bookbag, pulling out three shining bottles. He passed one each to Connor and Lisa.

"Cheers. To the end of the world!"

Glitch clinked bottles with Connor and Lisa.

Connor's mouth fell open. Main Hall was about to collapse, but what Glitch had just done seemed way weirder.

"This is *Double-Up Potion*," Connor said aloud. "You glitched this from the Potions Machine, didn't you? But wait. That would mean—" his voice slowed for a moment, then rose in a shrill squeak. "*Your bookbag can store* GLITCHED ITEMS *now?*"

"Actually, it's more of a *hack*." Lisa and Glitch shared a grin.

Connor's lips sputtered. He tried to form words, but the ceiling had already snapped.

The VGL world turned to white.

24
SPEED RUN

THE NEXT FEW MINUTES WERE A BLUR OF activity. Lisa took charge straightaway, so that Connor began to feel as if he were cruising along on an airplane.

Then JUMPING OUT OF the airplane.

"Lisa, what are you — OW!"

Connor let out a wail. No sooner had Ms. Vickers's chalk scraped the blackboard than Lisa jumped to her feet, raising their anvil-sized poem book.

BANG. She slapped Connor's chest with it.

THUMP. Then she tackled him!

"MISS Q.!" cried Ms. Vickers. "What is the meaning of — MY WORD! THE PRINCIPAL'S OFFICE, BOTH OF YOU!"

Eight seconds later ...

"OWWW!"

Connor let out *another* wail. The teleporter had just zapped their avatars to Main Hall. But as Connor stuck his two-footed landing, a heavy weight crashed on top of him.

"Finally, a nice trampoline!" Lisa bounced to her feet like a spring. "I *knew* a fake fight would work. Teachers hate fights — and they always punish both people!"

Connor crawled to his feet with a moan.

"Oh, get tough. You're up next!" Lisa flashed a wicked grin. Throwing Mr. Oldentone's door wide, she launched herself into the gap.

She froze instantly.

"Someone's taking this speed run a little too seriously," Connor grumbled.

Then he stopped himself. This was *their last loop.* If they failed now, there wouldn't *be* any VGL to go back to. So who was the unreasonable one, really?

Connor inhaled a breath.

He drew the Wolf Buster Sword out of storage. With a sudden grin (not unlike Lisa's) he charged down the hallway.

He had a Level 2 Slime to meet.

That poor fiend. It was doomed!

• • • ● • ● • • •

TEN MINUTES LATER, CONNOR returned to Main Hall with his best friend in an arm lock.

"Connor! Ow! Can you not—?"

"It's for your own good, Glitch."

There was a slight tussle, won by Connor, and soon Glitch was extending his Vid-Glove. The messed-up pixels in Mr. Oldentone's doorway began to shake.

There were loud hisses. Strange bleeps. Even staticky cracks.

But loudest of all was a slurping sound.

FWOOP.

As Glitch's avatar stiffened, Lisa emerged with a pop. She looked at Connor. They both winced.

It was an unfortunate truth that their speed run involved sending Glitch into a sort of black hole. Every loop he spent long hours trapped in his locker. This was easy to forget, because to

Connor and Lisa, it felt as if only a few seconds passed.

"Just a heads up," Connor told Lisa, "I didn't explain the time field to Glitch. It seemed faster that way. And, uh, he may or may not have been pushed through that doorway."

Lisa's face brightened. "Swift *and* ruthless. You're learning!"

A sudden "WHOOOOAAAAA!" rose from the doorway, followed by Glitch himself, screaming in terror.

"I've got this," said Lisa, as Connor leapfrogged his friend's rolling avatar. There wasn't time to explain. He had bigger things to worry about.

BANG!

The time field collapsed and Connor rushed forward. He spread his palms, found the invisible walls that appeared and began shimmying upward. He sped toward the now-floating doorway.

Glitch watched him go with wide eyes.

"IS CONNOR A GHOST NOW? HE FLOATS?"

"Keep climbing, I'll handle him!" Lisa yelled up to Connor.

She had already summoned a Vid-Screen.

· · · ● ◉ · ◉ ● · ·

INSIDE THE OFFICE, CONNOR fixed on a shimmering, molten gold light.

The Gold Disinfectant.

Connor slowly approached. *I'm a Custodian now*, he reminded himself. *I can just grab the bottle. Of course I can.*

So why was he walking on tiptoes?

How come his heart thumped relentlessly?

Connor's eyes slid to the dusky orb that loomed in the background. He stared nervously. When he was sure the Wisp wasn't in, he leaned all the way forward, extending his arm toward the bright, flutelike bottle.

His fingers closed around it. A lemony warmth flowed through his avatar.

"Wow," Connor whispered — *and phew*, he thought privately.

He had done it. There had been no alarm. No low, rumbling voice. No Sir William.

Connor winked at the Wisp's dusky orb. Stashing the bottle in his Vid-Glove, he turned heel and left the room at a sprint.

And a dive.

25
SPEED RUN, PT. II

THUMP.

"WARNING! Health reduced by thirty percent," said a voice.

"Ow," Connor echoed. He had jumped instead of climbed, and the crash landing *hurt*.

Worth it, thought Connor. Speed was everything.

Or was it?

A quick glance around the hallway island found Lisa and Glitch — who had only just started digging!

"I told you, copy the video," Lisa was saying.

Beside her, a Vid-Screen showed a recording of Glitch from a previous loop. His Vid-Glove arm did a funny wiggle.

"Is that a rain dance? I look like a *clown*," Glitch complained.

"You said that last loop. Just do it, okay?"

"This is freaking me out," Glitch grumbled.

But he wasn't grumbling for long. Goofy or not, the move worked. Under Lisa's instruction the hole in the floor grew steadily bigger, until a short wave from Glitch could send pixels blasting out of the ground. It was almost magical, watching their progress.

Unless you were Connor, that is.

"Hurry up," Connor groaned.

He paced the island impatiently. The wait was unbearable — like an unskippable cutscene in a video game. Connor almost regretted skipping the Custodial World on this loop. Without it, he was simply too quick.

Feeling bored, Connor checked his Quest Log again, then scrolled through his inventory.

I wonder, he thought suddenly.

He tapped his Vid-Glove. A lemony warmth filled his palm.

GOLD DISINFECTANT

Type: Relic

Rarity: S

Duration: 120s

Additional Information: So you want to battle a fiend past your level? Jump ranks with VGL's deadliest Cleansing solution. Tough on stains. Tougher on messy opponents!

Apply to the surface of any Cleaning Weapon to boost its base Attack by up to ten times. Effect varies by function.

"Rarity: S?" Connor's jaw dropped. Was Rank S even rarer than A? How was that possible? What *was* this stuff?

Suddenly loud voices rose from the tunnel.

"Stop pushing, Lisa. I'm not finished!"

"Come *on*. You're slower than the water cycle! I see the exit hole already. Punch through!"

"Not yet. I have to clear the right side still. Can you play my recording again?"

"No, we're already late. Stop time-wasting, Sven!"

"Don't call me Sven!"

"Forget it. I'll clear the exit my—AAARRGGH!"

Lisa gave a strangled yell. Connor's eyes widened. He banished the item with a wave. Then he leapt down the tunnel!

He found Glitch in a daze. And Lisa not at all. Sort of.

Connor counted one elbow, two knees and a tuft of willowy hair. The rest of Lisa's avatar was wedged inside the tunnel wall.

"I warned her," said Glitch. "The pixels on the right side are funky. Now she's trapped worse than me in my locker. Oh man. I hope I left a note about unsticking avatars ..."

A Vid-Screen shimmered beside him.

"Glitched items can also have glitched stats," said a hologram Glitch. "Most of the time that's annoying. But sometimes you can use a glitched item in ways the VGL world never intended. Take this bookbag, for instance ..."

Connor stared in amazement. "You recorded video lectures — *for your future self?*"

"Uh, I guess so?" Glitch smiled sheepishly. Then a tuft of Lisa's hair brushed his ear and he screamed.

Connor peered through the unfinished exit hole. "So if we keep left, we can leave?" he asked.

Glitch nodded. He stepped aside to let Connor pass.

"You go, Connor. There's a big enough gap if you're careful. I'll work on unsticking Lisa."

"You're not coming?" said Connor.

Glitch shook his head. "I may not be a time-looping weirdo like you guys—" he smiled weakly, "but I know how it feels being stuck. Plus I owe her one. Plus two, she owes *me*. I know she's hiding more lectures. Plus three, it's *Lisa*. If something goes wrong, we might need her."

Connor couldn't argue with that. He edged around Glitch, who began to offer a fist bump, then stopped.

"Better not," the boys agreed.

Connor rose through the exit hole. He emerged in front of Main Hall's side exit.

"Good luck!" Glitch called up.

"See you after class," Connor grinned.

26
SPEED RUN, PT. III

IT WAS PAST NINE O'CLOCK, AND CONNOR was running full out.

Nine fifteen, his mind kept repeating. *That's my deadline.*

He had about ten minutes to find Mr. Oldentone and deliver the Gold Disinfectant. Would the S-Rank item be enough to repel the Fanged Slime?

Connor didn't know.

Right now, his main concern was reaching the VGL Mainframe. According to Lisa, this meant taking the dangerous, twisting route that led beneath the land bridge shortcut. Which, in turn, meant crossing the Armorer's Tent.

A tent overflowing with lava!

Or was it ice now?

I can't remember. Was I supposed to remember?

Connor gulped. He had a sinking feeling he'd forgotten something.

"OWWW!"

Two steps from the tent, Connor's feet sizzled. His Vid-Glove gave a warning shake.

ALERT! BURNING GROUND!
Health will decrease without proper equipment.

Connor looked down. Lava flowed past his ankles. He yelled and hopped sideways—

"OWWW!"

This time, his feet crunched on ice! His Vid-Glove shook again.

ALERT! FROZEN GROUND!
Health will decrease without proper equipment.

"WHAT! What do I do?" Connor wailed.

Angry waves chased him higher. He climbed a hill near the tent and looked down. Waves of lava and frost swirled below. That's when it hit him.

"Level 5 boots! I don't have them!"

Connor uttered a moan. The boots were Lisa's specialty. He couldn't reach the Mainframe without them. His Hit Points would plummet!

I should've stayed and helped Glitch, Connor thought miserably. *With my help, we might've saved Lisa by now. Then I wouldn't be trapped on this miserable—*

"Huh?"

Connor's feet skidded. He looked down and gasped. The tiny hill, it turned out, wasn't solid. It was made of slipping and sliding junk items!

The armorer's junk heap.

A pair of swords on Connor's right hit the lava and melted. A helmet on his left filled with frost.

Connor shuddered. He wondered which would hurt worse, burning or freezing. He and Glitch used to joke about stuff like that.

Not anymore.

Icy hot waves sprayed his ankles. Ascending to the highest point possible, Connor looked around and yelled, "Lisa! Glitch! Are you out there? Come on, guys! If you're listening, this is the part where you—"

CRACK.

The item supporting Connor broke free. It was big and round, and as it slid toward disaster, Connor slid with it. Using his reflexes, he swayed like a surfer. But he screamed like Glitch on a haunted hayride.

"AAAAHHHHHH!" Connor shrieked.

Beneath him, the item squelched horribly. It had a disgusting half-metal, half-furry texture, reminding Connor of a rotted mushroom.

Wait. Glitch's shield? Was this the shield Glitch had touched?

A text box rose over the junk heap.

```
*@(Q*&$Y(ASF, LVL &^
Type: L*328SDFJI&^&*
Rarity: L?SF?ES?E*8
Durability: I*#@NS))S&@+
```

The stats were totally glitched!

Hang on. Connor's eyes narrowed. He recalled the words from Glitch's lecture:

Glitched items can also have glitched stats. Most of the time that's annoying. But sometimes you can use a glitched item in ways the VGL world never intended.

Connor stared at his feet. "I'm surfing ... on a shield," he said aloud. His mind jolted.

Every item at VGL had a type and a function. Most items were flexible. You could do *all kinds* of stuff with a pencil, for instance. But battle items were different. You had to act within their preset parameters. Shields, for example, couldn't double as sleds. Not normally.

But was a glitched shield really normal?

SPLASH. The fuzzy shield hit the lava. It bobbed instead of melting, while a friendly wave sent it skimming toward the Armorer's Tent.

"YEAH! LET'S GOOO!" Connor whooped.

Then his voice cut off as a second wave knocked him into the air. He stumbled and barely held on, landing hard in a funnel of steam, only to be launched up again — and *again*.

Crossing into the tent, Connor wasn't whooping anymore. He cried:

"W-W-WHOOOAAAAAHHH!"

27

LANDSLIDE

IF ANYONE WAS STILL ALIVE IN THE Armorer's Tent, they must have been cupping their ears.

Connor's screams never stopped. He screamed past the boot racks. He screamed between armor displays, even as he slalomed between them, and he screamed again ducking under a table.

Faster by far than the Level 1 Rusty Sled, the furry shield streaked down the aisles. It took all of Connor's skill to stay upright.

BANG.

A curling red wave hit the shield. Steam hissed as Connor did a limbo bend backwards. Swerving expertly, he carved down the edge, blasting out of the spray at top speed. And then—

"W-W-W-WHOAAAHHH!"

Connor gave his loudest scream yet. The lava had turned to thick ice!

Connor dropped to his knees, and then onto his stomach. The fuzzy shield whirled like a top, and Connor clung desperately. Eyes swimming, he crashed through the exit flap, past a large wooden sign ringed with frost.

THE LAND BRIDGE SHORTCUT
"Bridging" the gap between Lake Blessed and Fiend Fountain.

CAUTION! GUARDRAILS MISSING!

Do not use mobility items. Do not stray from the path. You have been warned, traveler!

The land bridge was exactly as advertised. Like a rope or a spear, a thin strip of land extended across a vast chasm — a sort of bottomless pit in the middle of campus.

How deep did the chasm go? What type of fiends lived there? And how was the chasm formed, anyway?

No one knew for sure. Kids who'd flown on airships or moon shuttles said the chasm, as seen from above, resembled a footprint. Giant creatures once roamed the VGL campus, they claimed.

But Connor knew better. Well, *Lisa* knew, and she'd shown them Vid-Screen recordings. Hidden deep inside the chasm was a rich vein of crystal. The crystal was a visual representation of energy, or power, or *something*. Whatever it was, the VGL Mainframe relied on it.

And the Fanged Slime planned to drain it away!

Connor tightened his grip on the shield. His Level 2 avatar might be weak, but he was a Custodian now. It was his duty to sweep fiends off of campus.

He *had* to enter the chasm. He had to finish his Quest and deliver the Gold Disinfectant to Mr. Oldentone, no matter how deadly the task was — or how terrified *he* was.

"Slooowww doowwwnn!" Connor begged.

The spinning shield veered toward a cliff. Connor's heart thumped. Thinking fast, he threw his weight all the way left and then all the way right. The shield sputtered and groaned, but it matched Connor's movements. It swung side to side like a serpent — which caused a *new* problem. The heavy turns put Connor at constant risk of flying off the edge.

Students had fallen before. They all died.

The drop was simply too huge!

Where's the path? Where's the path?

Connor's eyes swept the ice, searching for the twisting path off the bridge labeled "FORBIDDEN PASSAGE."

"It *can't* be," said Connor.

A nasty turn loomed ahead. Connor's mind screamed a warning, but his muscles were braver. A mighty swerve sent him crosswise, onto a spiraling route that veered off the shortcut.

BOING.

Connor bounced upward. He landed hard on his shield, only to find an ugly blue lump in his path. He tried to dodge. But more lumps appeared. They made slurping sounds, leaking lines of blue liquid across the ice.

Slimes? Were these Slimes?

BOING.

A second lump flung him higher. The shield creaked as it flew, soaring over the path, which turned sharply, and into the chasm beyond.

"Noooo!"

Wind whipped at Connor's avatar. Desperate, he clung to the shield like a life raft. And maybe it was. Could the glitched shield also act as a parachute? A hang glider?

"Please, please," Connor prayed.

The shield gave a worrying hiss. Lisa's words suddenly echoed in Connor's head:

Their slime is toxic! It can eat through most Sword types.

"And Shields tooooooo!" Connor yelled to the wind. A moment later, his last fuzzy handhold dissolved.

He plunged down the chasm.

28
HIDDEN SECTOR

CONNOR'S CHEEKS FLOPPED LIKE LEAKING balloons. It was a straight drop. The only difference between himself and a bungee jumper was the rope that wasn't strapped to his—

"Whoaaa!"

Connor's avatar jerked upward. Gravity settled and, quite remarkably, he found himself dangling by a rope in mid-air.

"What the—?" said Connor.

Beams of light swirled around him. They looked like glowing ropes, wrapping Connor in a sparkling cocoon. He was instantly reminded of the light strands in Ms. Vickers's classroom, the ones that were supposed to zap him to Principal Norris's office.

A wall of text shone through the ropes.

—Clearance Requested to HIDDEN SECTOR
—Verifying credentials ...
—Verification failed!
—Initiating BOOT protocol!

Uh oh, thought Connor. His body tingled. The beams of light flashed from yellow to red.

—BOOT protocol active!
—User "LAMB, CONNOR" identified!
—Accessing user memory ...
—Modifying memory ...

"Owww!" Connor felt an awful squeezing sensation, as if his brain were a cow being milked. He shut his eyes. Then a tone sounded, and the pressure relaxed.

—BOOT protocol interrupted!
—Verification disabled by root user "GINEVRA"
—Verification will not apply to user class "ALL"
—BOOT protocol ended!

—Verification complete!

—Access granted to HIDDEN SECTOR (VGL MAINFRAME)

"Root user ... 'GINEVRA?'" Connor read aloud.

Who was that? Some sort of system administrator? One of VGL's engineers? But then why would they disable security protocols for "ALL" users, and not just themselves?

This was a security check, right? That's what the ropes were? And BOOT protocol?

Speaking of which, hadn't the protocol ended? So how come he—

WHOOSH. There was a rush of wind. The light beams released, and suddenly Connor was falling.

Again.

"Whooaaaahh!" he cried out.

But soon his cries turned to gasps. As though lowered by golden ropes, his avatar began a slow drift down the chasm below.

He crossed a threshold of darkness.

ZZZZ!

Space tore, and Connor stared in amazement. He found himself looking down at the mouth of an enormous stone cavern. The walls twinkled, as pretty as stars, and deep cracks in the uneven floor exposed hunks of crystal as wide as Fiend Fountain.

Connor drooled a little. He almost wished he had a pickaxe in his inventory. The crafting potential alone!

Drifting lower, however, Connor felt his eyes start to ache. The light from the crystals was blinding. Overwhelmed, he found a dimmer part of the cave to rest his eyes on.

The crystals here were wet with blue liquid.

A *whole lot* of liquid.

Suddenly the liquid bounced up. There were loud slurps as it dived off the crystals. A silver broom swiped the space it had left. The air crackled. The broom rose again. This time, the liquid countered with a swat of its gelatin hand.

There was an eruption of energy.

BANG!

Connor's heart quaked. He didn't need the buzz of his Vid-Glove to know what was happening.

The Fanged Slime — Mr. Oldentone —

The final fight had begun!

29

THE FINAL BATTLE

THERE WAS A HITCH.

As battle raged below, Connor ... *drifted*. He swung his weight around, trying to steer toward the action.

"Hurry up, I'm on deadline!" he cried.

Nothing worked. No matter how much he shouted, or wriggled, or kicked, he continued to sink at the same glacial pace. He felt like the world's biggest snowflake.

Down below, silver and blue rang together. Mr. Oldentone was in constant motion. Raising the silver broom, he deflected a jet of blue liquid one moment, then countered the next. There were *pops* as his bristles transformed, at one point erupting with an arc of purple flame that seared a line across the Slime's liquid belly.

"Wow," Connor whispered.

The move had a drawback, however. Hanging over the battlefield, Connor had a sniper's-eye view of the Slime as its belly burst open. Blue liquid slopped to the floor. The heavy drops rose to form quivering mounds.

The mounds sprouted fangs.

They showed blazing red eyes!

Mr. Oldentone grimaced. Short sweeps of his broom drove the tiny Slimes back, but there were *so many*. Like zombies, they rose again and again while, behind them, the lead Slime buried its fangs in a fresh hunk of crystal. Its blue body swelled and enlarged.

"It's leveling up," Connor moaned.

Mr. Oldentone had dropped to one knee. "Good — trick," he gasped. "But you won't win. I know who sent you!"

The lead Slime looked up. "FEED, FEED," said its muggy voice. It returned to the crystal.

"No! That is not your desire!" Mr. Oldentone bellowed. "Those are Ginevra's words. You are being Corrupted!"

There was a *thwack*. A mighty sweep sent the Slime army reeling. The Custodian rose with a scowl, his eyes fixed on the lead Slime. Was he preparing a final assault?

THUMP.

Connor's feet hit the uneven ground. His landing was poor, and his timing was tragic.

Nine fourteen, said the clock.

Connor broke into a run.

"Mr. Oldentone! Mr. Oldentone!"

The Custodian's bald head whipped around. Connor tapped his Vid-Glove. In a burst of inspiration, he reared back with his arm, yelling, "CATCH!"

The Gold Disinfectant soared through the air. Connor's eyes tracked its dizzying flight. They didn't need to; the throw had been perfect.

Like a spiraling football, the bright, flutelike item sank toward Mr. Oldentone's outstretched arms — and slipped between them.

SMACK.

Mr. Oldentone howled in agony. He dropped both bottle and broom, clutching the lump lifting out of his forehead.

A shadow flashed across the rocks. Connor watched in horror as a jelly hand the size of a treetop shot out. It struck the staggered Custodian, dousing him in toxic blue liquid.

Mr. Oldentone stiffened. His wide eyes stared like a statue.

There was a moment of stunned silence.

"I would've caught that," Connor mumbled. He slid to a halt as his Vid-Glove pinged loudly.

QUEST LOG UPDATED!

Congratulations! Sort of? You successfully delivered item "Gold Disinfectant" to Mr. Oldentone, the Custodian! But how can a *statue* use a rare S-Rank item?

Like this Quest, the show must go on. The VGL world is at stake! Look around. Is there another Custodian who could handle this item? Hmm. You'd better hurry ...

Defeat the enemy Slimes. Save the school or die trying! Don't look at me, kid. Did you think the Custodian role was that simple?

There was a BOING. Mr. Oldentone's avatar shot skyward. His blue body shrank as it soared, fading into the clouds with a twinkle.

The Slime army roared savagely. Eyes blazing, they rounded on Connor, who stumbled back.

"Uh ... uh ... uh ..."

His heart hammered. Forget the Quest! He couldn't defeat the Slime *army*, much less the lead Slime that had already—

"Oww!"

Connor's heel bumped an item. He spun around. The item vaulted into the air. Connor caught it smoothly, felt the stiff bristles and stared in amazement.

OLDENTONE'S BROOM, LVL ??
Type: Cleaning / Spirit Weapon
Rarity: UNIQUE
Durability: B

Additional Information: The Custodian's Broom. For the ultimate clean, by all means required! Level determined by avatar. Renamable. Spirit bond strongly encouraged.

ALERT! ITEM OF DESTINY!
You have touched upon a fragment of Suu, the Transformer! This item cannot be exchanged, traded or transferred by normal means. It moves by Suu's will alone. So how did *you* get it, anyway?

"Spirit Weapon? *Item of Destiny?*"

Connor turned the broom in his hands. He felt an eerie jolt. A sudden *wrongness* swept through his avatar.

His mind reeled. He could not even think!

Meanwhile, the Slime army uttered a war cry. They rushed at Connor, who waved the broom end erratically.

"Uh ... uh ... *Explodio! Firebreatheus!*" he said at random.

It had absolutely no effect.

"Think, think," Connor pleaded.

He could not. A strange fog had invaded his mind. He clutched the silver broom tighter.

[Stop that! I am not a lemon you squeeze, boy!]

"WHAT!?"

Connor's eyes flew open. The low, rumbling voice had spoken *from inside his head.*

The silver broom started shaking. Connor stared down the pole. Anchored in front of the bristles, blazing like a torch in the night, was ...

"An orb? An emerald orb?"

Connor's voice sputtered.

"SIR WILLIAM?"

30
SPIRIT BOND

CONNOR DASHED ALONG THE CAVERN wall. The strange fog had cleared. He was fully alert now.

Unfortunately, so was Sir William. Forget the Slime army. The Wisp was waging a war *in his mind.*

[Who told you my name? Did you plot Oldentone's downfall? Are you a broom thief? An orb hunter? A HACKER? Speak, boy, or by Suu's light I swear, when my powers return, I shall—]

"Punish my insolence," Connor echoed. "We've met," he explained hastily.

[Lies! You are addressing Sir William, the All-Knowing Wisp. Keeper of facts. Guardian of all things Custodial. My mind is a steel trap! If we had met, I could NEVER forget.]

"If you say so," said Connor.

He swung the silver broom at a Slime. The pole flexed more than the Beginner's Broom he was used to, turning his sweep into a sort of wobbly poke.

BANG. The Slime exploded on impact.

"*Whoa!*" said Connor.

Sir William made a tutting sound. [A forward thrust? Who trained you, a unicorn? You wield a fragment of Suu, the Transformer as though it were a tree branch in danger of snapping!]

Connor gritted his teeth. He swung the broom a dozen more times, changing grips, adjusting his footwork, and trying to predict how the springy pole liked to move.

His first swings were wild. If not for the broom's innate power, the Slimes would have already triumphed. But Connor kept pushing. He sensed a breakthrough approaching.

Sir William, however, did *not*.

[Great Suu, is this truly my fate? I could move mountains once. Fiends groveled at my feet-equivalents. Now look at me. Bonded to some sniveling, low-level brat — an imposter with no training, no respect, no knowledge at all of the—]

BANG.

Connor gave a whoop as his front sweep connected. Then he dropped low and shifted to Leaf Blower, blasting a row of Slimes with a whirling tornado.

[SACRED BROOM ART! THAT WAS THE SACRED BROOM ART!]

Sir William's shock raised a puff of green smoke.

[WHO ARE YOU?]

Connor let his broom do the talking. He launched three new attacks in succession. His smile grew wide as the Slime army flew backward again and again.

Now *this* was battle! This was what joining Swords Team had been all about!

Swords Team.

Connor hesitated. He had almost forgotten.

[Boy, snap out of it! This is not a Custodial Arts exhibition. While you prance about, the *big* Slime is draining us dry. Sweep your way to the crystals before it's too late!]

"Oh. Right."

Connor's eyes cast around. The lead Slime was unmissable. It was twice Connor's height now, and *much* wider. Flush with power, its blue body shone brightly.

Brighter still were its eyes. Crimson light lit the cavern walls, outshining even the crystals. Suddenly the eyes shifted. They fixed on Connor, who raised his broom against the blazing red tide.

[Behold, the eyes of Ginevra. That is no ordinary Slime. There is Corruption here. Stay close. I am attempting analysis.]

A text box appeared.

Analysis Complete. Beginning Report ...

FANGED SLIME, LVL 16
Type: Gelatinous
Power: C
Speed: C
Defense: E

"Level 16?" said Connor. "As in one and six? *Double digits?*"

Sir William said nothing.

"Hello? How are we supposed to fight that thing? I'm Level 2! I don't even have a full health bar!"

The emerald orb darkened.

[You cannot fight it. The gap in levels is *seismic.* It is the difference between clouds and mud! Even if Ginevra does nothing, the Fanged Slime alone is almost ten times your level.]

Almost ten times ...

Connor's mind jolted. Without a word to Sir William, he turned heel and launched himself across the rocks, toward the bright, flutelike item that lay there, forgotten.

• • • ● • ● • ● • •

[POWER! UNLIMITED POWER!]

Sir William's voice was a glorious roar.

[Oh, the Great Suu is merciful! I rise to greatness. Soon my powers shall be fully — WHAT HAPPENED?]

Connor wiggled the bottle. A last golden drop trickled onto the broom. The Wisp snatched it greedily. Steam hissed from his orb, which nearly popped from its bracket, while the rest of the broom flashed a shimmering gold color, giving it an aura of invincibility.

[MORE! I NEED MORE!]

"Sorry, that's all I got." Connor tossed the empty bottle into the air. There was a sound like a sigh. The S-Rank item dissolved.

Sir William was thunderstruck.

[That was — GOLD DISINFECTANT? A brat like you obtained not just Oldentone's Broom, but a RELIC? And you actually USED it?]

Connor grinned. "I just boosted our Attack by ten times. The broom's power is based on my avatar, right? I know I'm just Level 2. But with the boost, can't I hit like I'm Level 20 now? That dopey Slime is just Level 16. We can squash it!"

The Slime bared its fangs in a hiss.

Somehow, Sir William hissed even louder.

[You fool! Given the same boost, *that dopey Slime* would bust through the level cap! Can your puny brain comprehend the Attack of a *Level 160* fiend? A single palm strike could shatter the world, and every avatar in it!]

Sparks flew from the Wisp's shaking bracket.

[Brat, the Gold Disinfectant is the Custodian's ultimate trump card! Its might is without equal. And yet you, in your infinite wisdom, cast its legendary, single-use, ten-times Attack boost — on a weapon controlled by A LEVEL 2 AVATAR! It makes my spirit core weep. Not even *Ginevra*—]

"Okay, fine, I get it," Connor said irritably.

He was sick of Sir William's lectures. They were wasting time.

9O seconds ...
89 seconds ...
88 seconds ...

The spell clock was ticking down. Connor's Attack boost would not last forever. Like most spells in the VGL world, its effects would expire, and quickly.

Connor looked up at the enemy Slime. Its evil eyes appeared glazed and out of focus. Ignoring Connor, it leeched the light from a row of bright crystals.

Was it distracted? Or was it laying a trap?

We're about to find out, Connor thought.

He raised the boosted broom over his shoulder.

He was already running.

31
FIEND CORE

ACROSS THE ROCKS. OVER THE RIDGE LINE.

As Connor sped toward the cavern, the Slime stretched lazily across the rocks. It looked almost defenseless: an enormous blue blob with its fangs sunk in crystals.

But Connor wasn't fooled. He knew that, any moment, that blob could lash out with a gelatin fist. How fast would it reach him? Could he dodge in time?

It doesn't matter. I still have to try, Connor thought.

Sir William seemed to reach the same conclusion. He had stopped badgering Connor and begun to give tips and advice.

In his own special way.

[Your dopey Slime has reached Level 17, boy. *Incoming.*]

A jelly palm lunged at Connor. He dodged frantically, while a blast of Leaf Blower sent the palm fizzing off course. There was a *bang*. The boulder behind him exploded.

[It grew again, boy. Level 18.]

"What! How is it growing so fast?"

[Heh. Apart from the obvious, it seems to have reabsorbed the Slime army. Too bad. At least *they* were foes you could beat.]

A second palm fizzed toward Connor, who felt a rush of panic. It was too late to dodge. He raised his broom in desperation. The golden pole met the palm strike head on—

BANG. There was an eruption of jelly.

"YES!" Connor whooped. The boosted attack left him grinning.

[Don't smile yet. You may pack a wallop for now, but you are the *definition* of a glass cannon. One bump and you'll shatter. You must not be hit! Now close the distance. Aim for the fiend core!]

Connor hesitated. "Uh, the fiend core?"

There was a growl.

[Boy, you deserve an S for incompetence! Every fiend has a fiend core hidden on its body. It is their weak spot. The exact location can vary. However, Gelatinous fiends make this easy. Watch its jelly. *There.* You see the dark lump?]

"I see it!"

[What a surprise. Now hurry. You must punch through the jelly and strike at the core. Only a clean hit will destroy it. But be warned: this Slime is not normal. I fear Ginevra's meddling.]

"Am I strong enough?" Connor asked.

[Brat, you'd better be. Go.]

The broom blurred as Connor closed the distance, dodging wet palms and arcs of blue liquid. His eyes fixed on the lump. At least six feet of jelly surrounded it.

The spell clock was ticking down.

15 seconds ...
14 seconds ...

FWOOSH. A jelly palm rushed Connor's avatar. But Connor was ready. From close range he rolled forward, ducking the palm with a somersault. As he rose, he aimed the broom like a spear.

POP.

He switched into Vacuum. A golden hose replaced the broom bristles. Connor drove it into the Slime. There were loud slurps as a hole opened up in the Slime's jelly.

Blue liquid rose in a wave.

Connor drew back his weapon. POP. He switched to Squirt Gun directly. A spray of hot water turned the wave into mist.

[Great Suu, that was awesome! Quickly, boy. Finish it! Finish it!]

Connor upped the pressure. The hot water thinned to a jet.

5 seconds ...
4 seconds ...

The Slime howled. Hot water drilled through the hole in its jelly. Connor clutched the shaking broom. It flexed with sheer blasting power, flashing silver and gold.

1 second.

There was a *pop*. An ugly lump, like an overgrown peach pit, tumbled out of the Slime. It flopped around in a pool of blue liquid.

[Destroy it!]

Connor's eyes glinted. "Time to finish this!" he cried, sweeping the broom in a swift downward—

WHOOSH.

An unseen force slammed his avatar! As if thrown by a hurricane, Connor flew backward into the air. He landed flat on his back.

"What's going on? What blocked me?"

Connor crawled to his feet. Looking back, he saw blazing red eyes.

The Slime was convulsing. Blue liquid rose in a cyclone. It spun in furious loops. There were loud hisses — staticky cracks — and when at last the storm ended, the Slime had tripled in size. It was no longer blue, but a hideous purple.

Its mouth was a slobbering pit. Bright fangs extended outward like tusks and a revolting fuzz lifted out of its jelly.

So did a dozen long tentacles.

"W-WHAT IS THAT?" Connor spluttered.

[*Ginevra.*]

Sir William uttered a curse.

Analysis Complete. Beginning Report ...

VAMPIRIC MOLD, LVL 20 [CORRUPTED]
Type: Gelatinous / Parasite
Power: B » S
Speed: C
Defense: B » S

ALERT! CORRUPTION IDENTIFIED!
An outside force is lending its power.
Battle not recommended!

A paralyzing fear swept across Connor's avatar. He felt spent, like a battery. He did not even scream as the tentacles jerked him into the air.

32
TEAMFIGHT

UP AND DOWN. DOWN AND UP. A SEA OF writhing tentacles tossed Connor from one to the next, using his screams for entertainment.

"FLY, FLY," said the Mold's muggy voice.

Oldentone's Broom had lost its molten gold luster. Its Attack boost had ended. So, too, had Connor's last hope of winning.

The Vampiric Mold was a titan. Rising sixty feet tall, it was a full Level 20, with Power and Defense raised to S, an almost mythical rank.

But how? How could it evolve like that?

Was this Ginevra's work? Was this the might of Corruption?

A wave of rotten-egg breath filled the cavern.

"What do you eat, *toilets*?" Connor gagged.

"FEED, FEED!"

A long tentacle grabbed Connor out of the air. It began to lift him toward the Mold's drooling mouth. A pair of crimson eyes cast a gloating look.

Ginevra.

Connor's heart shook. He was terrified!

Not of dying. He would *not* think of dying. Instead he thought of his old, offline school: a return to live classes — to being small and awkward again — to eating lunch from a brown paper bag at his locker, because where would he sit? And then *recess* ...

No Glitch to hang out with.

No Lisa to say, "Connor! You forgot *another* pop quiz?"

He wondered if he would see them again. They lived in different states, after all. How long would it take for the VGL world to crash? Could they have a last meeting, however brief, in detention?

Connor's Vid-Glove gave a warning shake.

"Critically Low Health," it announced, as the Vampiric Mold drew him closer. Its mouth was a deep hole to rival the chasm, except where a tongue wet with drool wiggled out.

The stench was overpowering now. Connor shut his eyelids. Should he summon Oldentone's Broom one last time?

No, he thought. There was no point pretending he—

BOOM.

The cavern walls trembled as a staticky *crack* rent the air. Suddenly the tentacle gripping Connor fell slack.

What? HOW?

Connor didn't know. He didn't care! Pulling free of the Mold, he found himself scrambling across a tentacle that appeared to be frozen in time.

"CONNOR!" cried a voice.

Connor looked down. Two figures were descending a stream of shimmering air. Glitch hit the ground first. As Lisa tapped furiously at a Vid-Screen, no doubt hacking the tentacles, Glitch broke into a fumbling run. His bookbag bounced wildly as he clutched at the zipper. It finally released with a hiss, then a *pop*, and suddenly bottles were launching into the air!

Connor dived across the tentacles. His arms blurred. He snagged bottle after bottle until he had enough Double-Up Potion to fill one of the high tables next to their ... *wait a moment.*

Déjà vu, Connor thought.

"Drink them!" roared Glitch.

Connor didn't hesitate. A warm feeling spread through his avatar, his digitized body; he drained Double-Up Potions the way that land guzzles water (before it eventually rises again in a cycle of condensation, transpiration, precipitation ...) until his Vid-Glove gave a glorious shake.

ALERT! Health bar already at maximum.
Your Hit Points did not double.

"Full health! I'm at full health!" Connor whooped.

The ground began to shake. A bursting sound rose from the Vampiric Mold's belly. Swaying as he stood on a tentacle, Connor looked down and saw a clump of purple fiends rush at Lisa.

Her fingers froze in mid-tap.

"Noo!" she shrieked. "Go away! Get them off!"

Meanwhile, the tentacles were stirring. With a jolt, Connor recalled Lisa's words.

I'm useless in battle. I can't type under pressure. I can't think!

Several tentacles were rising now. Connor watched them in horror. Without Lisa to freeze them, they would be on him in seconds!

"Glitch!" Connor yelled down. "Form a perimeter! Keep those tiny Molds off of Lisa. She can't hack with them there. She hates battles!"

"S-So do I!" Glitch spluttered. "I'm not a fighter! I can't even summon—" his voice halted; he looked down at his Vid-Glove, "*a weapon.*"

A light bulb seemed to go off in Glitch's head. Shutting his eyes beneath his swim goggles, he raised his arm and cried, "Aaaaaahhhh," charging the Molds with his Vid-Glove outstretched.

His balance was dreadful. He stumbled from rock to rock until his feet slipped and he lurched forward in dizzying circles, a ballerina of death.

BANG. BANG. BANG.

The Molds erupted on impact. Glitch's Vid-Glove was like a close-range explosive! Job done, he fell forward. His Vid-Glove arm immediately punched through a rock.

"Back online!" Lisa yelled.

But while the tentacles slowed their movements, they did not stop completely. Ginevra's red eyes were blazing. There were loud hisses and staticky cracks.

"Someone else is in the system! Another hacker!" cried Lisa.

"It's Ginevra!" said Connor.

"Who?"

"Just do your best! I'm going in for the kill!"

Lisa nodded. But Connor didn't — he cringed.

Going in for the kill? On a Level 20 Vampiric Mold?

But now that he'd said it, he had to try.

He jumped from tentacle to tentacle, racing toward the Mold's gaping mouth. The thick tongue seemed to jeer at him. It was a ghoulish bone-white, with an ugly lump at the tip.

Connor gasped. He summoned Oldentone's Broom with a wave.

[Boy, I admire your guts. There are brave men in this world. But it takes a real freak to want to die getting eaten.]

"Oh shut up." Connor pointed to the lump on the Mold's ghoulish tongue. "That's the fiend core, I recognize it!"

There was a pause.

[So it is. It seems Ginevra is teasing us. She leaves the fiend core exposed, knowing we cannot hope to strike it. I may be a Guardian, a living fragment of Suu, but my powers are limited by what *you* can do, boy. Which is practically nothing.]

"I could throw you," Connor suggested.

[Impossible. A Spirit Weapon cannot be thrown. At least, not by means you possess.]

"What about items?"

[You mean your glitchy friend? By all means, let us shower the fiend core with *healing potions*.]

"I didn't mean Glitch," Connor said slyly.

He sank his thoughts into his Vid-Glove. There was a *pop* as a token appeared in his palm, along with a message:

ABILITY TRIGGERED!
Custodian's Call, Lvl 1
Summon a cleaning token when you need one (cooldown: 3600s)

[BOY, YOU ARE FULL OF SURPRISES!]

Ginevra's eyes flashed with shock. But too late. The cleaning token was already airborne. It hit the Mold's ghoulish tongue tip and crumpled, filling its mouth with thick smoke.

CLEANING SPIRIT, LVL 3
Type: Minion
Skills: Purify, Lvl 3; Scour, Lvl 1
Duration: 60s

The Cleaning Spirit had green eyes and a swirling mouth. It hovered in place, using its swirling mouth in imitation of the Sacred Broom Art's Vacuum mode.

The low-level attack was useless against the Level 20 Vampiric Mold and its S-Rank Defense. The fiend core, however, had no such protection. The Cleaning Spirit swallowed it instantly.

Sir William's orb shook with glee. [Cousin of mine! Taught him everything!]

The Vampiric Mold gave a last bellow. Its tentacles drooped and its huge body swayed against a cavern wall, shrinking rapidly. Connor raced down a limping tentacle. He hit the ground just ahead of the Mold's final attack.

A belly flop.

Purple waves lifted into the air. Connor grinned as he shifted to Squirt Gun. The waves turned to mist. He had won.

"That was rude of you."

A trail of smoke lifted over the wreckage. Crimson eyes blazed to life. Beneath them, Ginevra's fiery lips formed a pout.

Oldentone's Broom began to shake. Sir William shot out of his orb, his emerald eyes glaring.

Ginevra sneered at him. "Of course it's *you.* Did you enjoy our little game, William?"

"You failed, Ginevra."

"*Did* I?" Ginevra's lips curled in amusement. "Your server was ravaged. How many resets did you waste? *All* of them, if my readings are right. You even spent one of your trump cards. How adorable. We have our own relics, of course. Ask Oldentone about them. Do send my regards. As for *you*, little squirrel—"

Connor felt a sudden pressure. He fell to his knees as Ginevra's red eyes pinned him down.

"This world is going to burn, sweetie. If I were you, I'd skip town. Or better still, *disconnect.*

Have you considered boarding school? I know a charming headmistress."

Connor scowled. He balled his fists and, for one shining moment, he surged to his feet.

Ginevra's crimson eyes flared.

"MINE!" she roared. "This server is MINE. The VGL world will be MINE. Hear me! My name is Ginevra, Plaguebringer! The All-Infecting! The Undying!"

She's even worse than Sir William, thought Connor. He was flat on his chest. Ginevra's gaze was like a mountain pressing down on him. Still, in a weak voice he mumbled:

"Your name is Ginny ... the Germ?"

The air trembled. "I AM GINEVRA!"

There was a blast of raw, violent energy. Crimson light shot to the ceiling. It burst through thick rock and rose higher, still higher, until the VGL world burned a hideous red.

Connor felt a wave of helplessness. Against power like that, who could fight? He wanted to curl up and hide. Even dying, he felt, would be nice. A long moment passed, and the pressure released. But not the memory.

Not the mark it had left.

33
REWARD

CONNOR ROSE AT A HOP. GINEVRA'S EXIT had rattled him — oh yes — but her sudden defeat left him giddy, almost manic.

"GG!" he cried, raising his arms.

Nothing happened. Connor cleared his throat loudly. "GG!" he repeated. "GG!"

No response again. *Seriously?*

Connor paced the cavern impatiently. Long rows of crystals shone brightly. That boded well for the Mainframe, right? Okay, so the ceiling had smashed, and pools of slime covered everything. But all of that could be fixed.

What more could a Quest ask of him, anyway?

Connor had defeated the Fanged Slime, then the Vampiric Mold. He'd saved the VGL Mainframe. He'd even fought off *Ginevra*, who was some kind of mega boss. So where were the fireworks? The Flux bombs? The loot shower?

Connor spread his arms in frustration.

"Nothing? That's all I get? *Really*?"

[Brat, you want MORE? You're luckier than a loot box already!]

There was a sudden wail. Connor turned to find Glitch struggling with his Vid-Glove arm. It was still stuck in the ground, leaving him helpless against the tiny Mold climbing up his left boot.

Glitch's legs fluttered madly. Finally the Mold lost its grip. It released with a *pop*, bouncing across the rocks up to Connor. He swept his broom out. There was a *squish*.

"A little help?" pleaded Glitch.

"Typical," said Lisa. But as she bent to offer a hand, there was a trumpeting sound.

The air in front of Connor erupted.

```
ENEMY DEFEATED!
VAMPIRIC MOLD, LVL 20 [CORRUPTED]
+ 9,031 XP, + 1,421 Flux
Drops: Spiked Bracer (x1), Gelatin (x6),
Moldy Tissue (x50)

QUEST COMPLETE!
```

Streams of XP and Flux swooped from the sky like great diving birds. They converged on Connor's avatar, and didn't stop for a very, very long time.

```
LEVEL UP!
LEVEL UP!
LEVEL UP!
LEVEL UP!
LEVEL UP!
LEVEL UP!
LEVEL UP!
```

· · · ● · ● ● · · ·

ON THE WAY UP the chasm, Connor couldn't stop boasting. Luckily Glitch was an eager listener, because Lisa was *not*. She was scanning lines of dreary security code, fixing it so the mysterious air would rise faster.

Connor thought that was pretty cool, actually. But he would have preferred a heads-up.

"Got it!" cried Lisa.

There was a *whoosh*, and Connor and Glitch suddenly shot up like cannonballs. Their avatars soared high above the land bridge shortcut, stalled out, then entered a steep dive toward the large wooden sign near the Armorer's Tent.

"WHOOOAAAAAAH!"

They crashed in a heap, then yelled again as Lisa landed on top of them. She used their backs like a springboard.

"Thanks," she giggled.

Connor groaned. Beside him, an angry Glitch opened his bookbag. He let loose with a seemingly endless spray of Double-Up Potions.

Lisa dodged them easily. "How dare you use my lessons against me!" she said. She laughed again, and everyone topped up their health bars.

"We glitched the Potions Machine to shoot from my bookbag," Glitch explained with a burp.

The Armorer's Tent was oddly calm as they entered it. The lava and ice had stopped flowing. Their effects had mostly dissolved by this point.

"Sure you don't want boots, just in case?" Lisa waved a pair of Level 5 boots at Connor.

He shook his head.

"Level 9, Lisa. I've got Hit Points for *days*."

Grinning, Connor summoned his Stat Sheet. Lisa might as well see it. He'd made Glitch look a dozen times already!

LAMB, CONNOR — STUDENT, LVL 9
Role: Custodian (Rank E)
Abilities: *Custodian's Call, Lvl 1*
Modifiers: + Speed, + Stamina, - Strength
Rank: B (#48 of 1000)

Lisa squinted. One of her eyebrows arched up. "Congratulations, Connor. You're famous."

She summoned a Vid-Screen. A list of VGL's highest-ranked students beamed across it. The name LAMB, CONNOR appeared in shining white text at the bottom: #48 out of 50.

A *Ranker.*

Connor and Glitch traded stunned looks. The Ranker list — they'd completely forgotten!

"A fourth-grade Ranker," Glitch said in awe.

Connor was speechless. He rubbed his eyes, peering closer. There was a *hiss*. Suddenly the screen blurred, and Connor's name disappeared from the list. The name ROCHA, MARI replaced it.

"*What!*" Connor's eyes swung to Lisa, who raised her hands in the air.

"Wasn't me," she said quickly.

There was a sudden *crack*. Connor spun around. Beside him, a suit of armor was shaking to life. Layers of hardened blue slime fell away.

"Mr. Oldentone!" said everyone.

The bald-headed Custodian had a Vid-Screen out. He made a last swipe and banished it.

"William's been filling me in," he said as Connor, Glitch and Lisa all stared. "You kids did good. I'm impressed. But for this line of work, you need to keep a low profile. Some Stat Sheets are better left hidden," he told Connor.

"*Busted*," said Glitch.

Connor shuffled awkwardly. He didn't really know Mr. Oldentone. He rarely interacted with teachers and staff.

"Uh, your broom, sir," said Connor. He drew the silver broom out of storage.

Mr. Oldentone shooed him away. "Yours. Couldn't take it back if I wanted to."

To demonstrate, he reached a hand out. Either he was an excellent actor, or an unseen force knocked his hand away.

Sir William flew out of his orb in a towering rage. "But — but he's a *child!*"

"Suu's rules, William, not mine. In any case, I have my own troubles." Mr. Oldentone drew up his sleeve. Pulsing red vines wrapped his Vid-Glove arm. "This wound is not simple," he explained. "It appears our side was not alone in using relics. The Enemy is raising the stakes."

"*Ginevra,*" Connor said at once.

Mr. Oldentone shuddered. "Let's just say there are forces at work that exceed even my understanding. I apologize, son. This world — in some ways, it is more real than virtual. And it is no place for kids. It was a great fool who first put a school here."

"I don't understand," said Connor.

"You will, son." Mr. Oldentone sighed. "Like it or not, you're a Custodian now. Even if you weren't, you've been marked by Ginevra. Your world is going to change. That goes for you two, as well." He glanced at Lisa and Glitch. "So what do you think? Want to protect the VGL world from devastation?"

"Are you *sure* you're the good guys?" said Lisa.

"Do we get weapons?" Glitch asked eagerly.

"To hear William tell it, you *are* the weapon," said Mr. Oldentone.

"William? Do you mean *Sir* William?"

There was a pause. Mr. Oldentone scratched his bald head. He glanced at the Wisp, who puffed with thick smoke.

"The weak should respect their superiors," said Sir William. "I regret nothing."

"I'm sure you don't," Mr. Oldentone said with a chuckle. "Now then, let's make things official."

He waved a hand. A text box appeared next to Lisa and Glitch.

ABILITY UNLOCKED!
Custodian's Ear, Lvl 1

Support Ability. Can receive @Custodian pings. No role required. Auto-Equip.

"Cool!" said Lisa.

Glitch stared in disbelief at his Vid-Glove.

"It worked … I actually gained an ability! I can feel it!"

He pumped his fists in delight. There was a sudden hiss. An arc of lightning sent Connor diving to the floor.

"Whoops," Glitch apologized.

There was one last bit of business. Mr. Oldentone led Connor, Glitch and Lisa down a winding path toward Lake Blessed. He had refused to say why. He was acting rather cagey, in Connor's opinion.

"Wait here," said Mr. Oldentone, trotting off.

"Why is everything such a mystery with this guy?" Connor grumbled.

Lisa went a step further. In a voice that resounded across the Lake Blessed shoreline, she said:

"There's one thing I don't get. We just spent dozens of hours in the VGL world, right? Well, I suppose everyone else did as well, though I'm not sure they noticed." She glanced at Glitch. "But what's going to happen when we *leave* VGL? Were we locked in our Immersion rigs the whole time? Will we sleep for a week? Or was it some kind of temporal anomaly, like what Pfluter predicts in his First Supposition? How much time has passed, *really*?"

Lisa put her hands on her hips, glaring across the shore at Mr. Oldentone.

"Oh lay off him, Lisa," said Glitch. "Who cares? I want to know what *that* is." He pointed to a funny swirl in the lake water.

Connor felt a strange premonition.

"*Get back!*" he said quickly. But there was no need. Suddenly everyone was scrambling backward as a large creature burst through the lake water. It had a dragon's long, scaly snout and a mane of glittering fish fins. Only its huge head was visible — yet, compared to it, the Vampiric Mold was a sugar plum.

"Evie," Mr. Oldentone explained. "One of our Guardians. Deep down she's just a big softie. Aren't you, Evie?"

A huge head bared its teeth. Connor, Glitch and Lisa backed further away as Mr. Oldentone and Evie made contact. There was some sort of item exchange — then a glimmer, a snort and an eerie, almost imperceptible splash.

Evie returned to the depths.

Mr. Oldentone trotted back up the shoreline. A strange cube hovered over his palm. It seemed to appear and disappear as it spun.

"*What is it?*" said everyone.

"A fair question," said Mr. Oldentone. But he did not explain.

He turned the cube in his hands. After a moment, something clicked. A Vid-Screen rose into the air. The screen looked *bizarre* — almost like something Glitch would come up with.

Connor tilted his head. No matter which way he turned, he could not see the contents.

"Ah, this one." Mr. Oldentone flicked a finger. The cryptic screen became visible. It said:

EMERGENCY POWER CELL
Charge Remaining: 1%
WARNING! DOES NOT RECHARGE!

Requires min. 5% charge to reset (automatic)

"Oof. William was right. You kids did a number on this power cell," said Mr. Oldentone.

"Sorry," said Connor. "No one told us the charge was limited. It's our fault the server is out of resets. We used them all fighting that Slime."

Mr. Oldentone arched an eyebrow. He seemed amused by something. As he scrolled down the screen, a final line appeared beneath the fold: a line which had escaped everyone's notice till now.

Requires min. 1% charge to reset (manual)

"Yes, Ginevra has been flushed from the server," said Mr. Oldentone, "but her Corruption runs deep. Who can say what *other* surprises she may have left for us? Indeed, it is best to be safe ..."

He scrolled further, beginning to type.

"Uh, guys? What's he doing?" said Glitch.

"I'm adding our names to the naughty list," Mr. Oldentone chuckled. "No mind wipe for us. Why should these two get to hog all the fun?"

He winked at Connor and Lisa.

"Is that button what I think it is?" said Lisa.

"Uh, it's big and red," Connor said nervously.

"Don't worry, the Slimes have been purged," said Mr. Oldentone. "As for you three ..."

A smile crept over his face. He pushed the flashing red button.

"Initiating Manual Reset," said a voice.

There was a hiss. Then a bleep.

Then a staticky *crack*.

34

AFTER CLASS

TWO FIFTY SEVEN.

Two fifty eight.

Two fifty nine.

Connor watched with bated breath. There was an agonizing pause as the clock neared the top of the hour. The second hand seemed to wobble unnaturally. There was a sudden click—

It moved backwards!

"WHAT!" Connor leapt out of his seat with a roar. But the final bell was already ringing. Students laughed and fled for the door.

"Gotcha," Lisa snickered. She banished her Vid-Screen and skipped out the door, ahead of Connor's grasping hand.

"I will see you all bright and early tomorrow!" Ms. Vickers announced. She poked her head out the doorway. "No crossbows in the hall, Ms. Mayes. You know the drill. Wait for practice — or better still, try a *real* sport. I recommend badminton!"

Out in the hall, Connor felt a sudden shove. He grunted and bounced off a wall. Looking back, he saw two boys pointing bright swords, which they'd summoned the moment Ms. Vickers had turned away.

"You're coming, right? Swords Team?"

"Better be. We need someone to wail on!"

The boys laughed and sped off, not even waiting for Connor's answer.

"I never liked those guys, anyway," Connor muttered.

He felt strange as he walked across campus. Wherever he looked, he saw student avatars. Most were headed to after-school sports. Others flashed rare gear and items, or were teaming up to craft recipes. Connor passed one such group. They had amassed twin mounds of rubber and steel, which blurred as a claw hammer struck them. A pogo stick emerged with a *pop*.

"Cool!" they said. "But ... who gets to keep it?"

Connor dashed ahead of the scuffle.

It seemed things had truly returned to normal. Even the Armorer's Tent had a lively crowd of avatars in attendance. Approaching Main Hall, however, Connor felt a spike of nervousness. He entered warily, then *slowly* approached the door labeled "CUSTODIANS ONLY," in case it suddenly leapt into the air or began launching pixels at him.

Neither happened. The door opened and Connor found Lisa and Glitch standing alone, inspecting long rows of cleaning supplies.

"Hey," said Connor. "Where's—?"

There was a *bang*. Mr. Oldentone came striding into his office, looking flustered. He waved a hand and a rather large map beamed to life. It showed a glowing red dot. Several, actually.

"Good, you got my ping. Something's come up, I'm afraid."

His eyes cast around.

"It's Ginevra."

ALSO BY SCOTT CHARLES

MYLO AND MAX BREAK THE WORLD
VIDEO GAME ELEMENTARY

THE FINAL INGREDIENT
THE BONE TAKER
THE BREAKING GAME

Looking for more *Video Game Elementary*? Never fear! Connor, Glitch and Lisa will return — and probably sooner than you think! To stay up to date, find me online at www.Scott-Charles.com and add your name to:

THE SCOTT CHARLES NEWSLETTER!

Get the knowledge you need to keep your virtual classroom secure, and *far* out of reach of Ginevra — or whomever else might come knocking. One thing's for sure: life at Video Game Elementary is about to get a lot more ... *interesting.*

ABOUT THE AUTHOR

SCOTT CHARLES is the author of *Video Game Elementary*, an epic adventure series for young readers, as well as the *Creeptown* series and the standalone adventure *Mylo and Max Break the World*. He writes thrilling books for busy kids who might not want to be reading, but what choice do they have? Zero! None!

Scott grew up in a pair of small towns outside of Princeton, New Jersey. He attended Duke University, where he graduated with a B.A. in Public Policy and successfully summoned [REDACTED]. He enjoys the spoils of his dastardly deal at his home in Charlotte, North Carolina. You can find him at the library, across a chess board, or on a soccer field late, late at night.

Made in the USA
Monee, IL
03 February 2022

90533573R00132